social code

By **CASS TELL**

Destinée S.A.

Published by Destinée S.A., www.destinee.ch

Cover design & Layout by Leigh Merchant

ISBN 0-9759082-0-0

social code

social code
Prologue

Pitbill stalked along the dark alley, his handgun ready. Silently skirting a large trash dumpster, he stopped. Checking the shadows, he stepped out onto the street.

A figure leapt in front of him, and in the same instant Pitbill pulled the trigger. He kept firing again and again, filling the air with the sound of rapid gunfire as the man's head exploded off his shoulders, blood spinning in the air. The headless body tumbled backward to land in a splattered sprawl at Pitbill's feet. Its severed head hit the curb, and rolled several feet along the gutter before stopping. The eyes remained open in short-lived surprise, staring up at the gray sky.

Pitbill wasted no time. One moment of inattention and they would take him out. He wasn't going to let that happen. Not after working so hard to achieve his goal. Above all he needed to control his emotions. Had he fired too many indiscriminate shots?

He continued down the street. Three thick, broad-shouldered men jumped out from behind a parked car and began firing in his direction. Pitbill fired back, hitting hearts and heads. Bodies exploded in front of him, spraying blood across the white parked car.

The red liquid ran down the windows and doors in jagged lines.

Moving forward again past the bodies, Pitbill saw the door. His heart stopped. This was it, the one he had been seeking. It would take him to the very highest level—once he passed the test.

The test might take days, even weeks, but Pitbill had been preparing for it. He was ready.

He opened the door to see a girl seated on a raised chair at the end of a long room. She looked no more than fifteen, her blond hair and ivory skin a translucent perfection. A transparent, filmy netting billowed over her fine slender body.

"Hello, Pitbill," the girl smiled. "Welcome to the final test. You have been an admirable warrior to make it here. Few do." She stood up in one swift shifting of limbs and fabric, revealing long slender legs. "Pitbill, are you ready to undertake the final challenge to become a Master Protector?"

"Yes, Angelica," Pitbill breathed.

"The test is considerable," Angelica stated, her computer-generated voice sounding almost real. "As was the case at previous levels, you will go through the door on the right. We will begin when you are ready. You have a three-month deadline to complete the test. If you do not complete the test by that time, you will have to return to Level Nine and redo it." She gestured at him with her arm and then at the door.

Pitbill moved to the right and entered the room.

Angelica smiled.

... **Chapter 1** ...

The same popup ad kept flashing on to Doby's screen. 'Buy Cheap Computer Gear Here.' The ad's link was to a website he had never visited and—because of the exasperating ad—never planned to.

Worse than that, his computer kept blocking, or rather stalling. The little hourglass icon appeared on the screen after every third or fourth click of the mouse, and the hard drive spun on.

Doby knew how to deal with popup ads. His concern was the slow machine.

He shoved back from his desk, sending himself backward on the wheeled chair. Another ad popped up and he was glad to be far enough away to be unable to read what it was advertising.

He reached for a printout from the long table that ran along a wall to his right. On the table sat another flat screen monitor, linked to a separate computer than the one with the popup ads. Not finding the papers he wanted, he slid over to another table. This one was stacked with technical reference books and piles of papers with napkins and magazines sticking out of several stacks.

At the end of the table was a disorderly pile of books on history, philosophy and economics, the overflow from a crammed bookshelf that covered one wall. A Bible in French was at the bottom of the pile and on top was a guidebook for the Uffizi Gallery in Florence.

Next to the guidebook was a notebook with some of his poems, or something more like prose reflections. He knew he wasn't very good at it, but occasionally he wrote down these expressions as an alternative form of creativity, other than dealing only with computer code. For a split second he considered writing down his feelings about the popup ads.

Finding his printout and then deciding not to bother with it, Doby took the last swig of cold coffee from a previous day's mug and glanced longingly at the cot in the corner. He had been up most of the night working, and a catnap would be . . . a waste of time. He grimaced at the condensed caffeine and rubbed his temples, shifting his 50's- style black-rimmed glasses up and down.

Luckily he was a computer engineer, and no hardware or software problem had stopped him yet. And though these problems were interesting and complex puzzles to solve, from experience he knew they could become real time killers.

Plus, he had far more important things to do than tinker with the computer. Just thinking of his slipping schedule made him edgy. And he wanted to get working on his new website, recently registered and very quickly developed, but not yet what he really wanted.

He swiveled to check on the flat screen television that he left on mute 24-7 to keep up with news and stocks. A commercial was running. He glided back to his terminal. Despite the frustrating nature of the problem, he admitted to being curious about it.

The spinning hourglass told him there was a program running somewhere on his machine. What was it and why was it slowing the machine down? And was it connected to the incessant popup ads?

There was no way in the world this computer should be running so slowly. Two weeks ago he had completed a major upgrade, a regular ritual he did with all his computers.

The computer now had a top-of-the-line processor and the

largest hard drive on the market. A lot of people would kill to have a PC with this much speed, yet now it was acting like an old plough horse.

... # ...

He did a quick hardware check and everything was in order. Must be a software issue.

As he checked through the software, the popup ads kept appearing, so he ran a cleanup program that found and deleted them.

It didn't work. That meant someone had found a way to conceal the popup software so that the detection program could not find it. And this meant several hours of work. Doby shook his head and then had to brush his hair back from his eyes. When was the last time he'd had it cut? He usually wore it short and tousled. Well, at least the tousled part still held.

He worked through a list of diagnostics, starting with basics like closing down all open applications. A more complex diagnostic program took an unusual amount of time to complete, but the ads kept on coming.

Perhaps some software program has gotten out of whack? he thought. It happened sometimes. *OK, reboot the thing,* he told himself.

He moved the cursor to the Start button and clicked the mouse, but nothing happened. The system was now blocked.

Ridiculous.

He reached down, put his finger on the on-off button and pushed. A hard stop—which he detested doing. In a moment the fan's whirring ceased. For a software engineer, having to turn off a

PC manually was like driving a brand new sports car in a destruction derby.

Feeling defeated, he turned the machine back on. It took a full ten minutes for the faulty computer to reboot when it should have taken only one or two. It's still there, he thought to himself, wishing he could throw the computer through the window, except that this basement room didn't have a window. Bomb shelters weren't designed for maximum daylight.

The popup ad reappeared.

Maybe a virus? That would surprise him. His anti-virus software was up-to-date. Nonetheless, he did a virus scan and started performing various other system checks. After forty-five minutes, one of his diagnostic programs finished and revealed something odd. A nonstandard code appeared to be imbedded into the operating system. It acted like a tumor, invading files that should never be touched. Puzzling. Uninvited code in the operating system was bad news. It meant expert software.

Doby leaned back in his chair and put his feet on a wobbly stack of papers at the edge of his desk, sending a sheet zigzagging through the air to the ground.

The fact that he had worked most of the night wasn't helping him to analyze the problem correctly. What was the answer?

"Coffee," he answered himself aloud. He tripped over a stray cable and headed up into the farmhouse kitchen.

... **Chapter 2** ...

It took several minutes for the coffee to brew, a rich Arabica from Kenya that he sourced from a local roaster. He poured himself a cup and walked out into the fresh Swiss air. It was a clear day and he enjoyed the view of fields and vineyards descending down to Lake Geneva. On the opposite side of the lake rose the Alps. Mont Blanc, Europe's tallest mountain, towered above the other peaks, white and shining.

But despite the Arabica and magnificent view, his mind stayed knotted to the rebellious computer downstairs.

He was just turning back toward the farmhouse when he heard the telephone ring. He hurried inside and picked up the cordless phone.

"Hello. Doby here," he answered in French.

"Hello Doby," a voice replied in the same language, "This is Stefan von Portzer."

Doby's heart skipped a beat. Stefan von Portzer owned this farmhouse, and Doby was doing some research for him, yet he wasn't making progress because of the computer problem.

"Hey. How's it going? Are you enjoying your holiday?" Doby asked. Stefan was calling from the Maldives where he had just gone off for two weeks with a lady friend.

"Absolutely. The warm air and blue water are just what I needed," von Portzer replied. A low, feminine voice in the background suggested to Doby that lovely landscape wasn't all von Portzer had needed. The woman's voice broke off into a soft laugh and Stefan continued, "I wanted to call to see how the research is progressing."

"Oh . . . good, but it's taking time." Von Portzer had asked Doby to investigate a businessman in Germany, to find out his real net worth as part of a business deal in negotiation. The German kept telling von Portzer that he didn't have enough money. Doby was asked to find out whether he did, which meant accessing some sensitive data. Initial investigations had revealed that the businessman was connected to the German underworld and he wondered what kind of deal von Portzer was working on. It was better not to ask.

"I would appreciate it if you could finish the investigations as soon as possible," von Portzer said, "I need to conclude the affair when I get back to Europe."

"When are you coming back?"

"In ten days."

"I'll do my best," Doby said, wondering if his best would be good enough.

"I know you will. Look. If you have any problems getting the information, just let me know, and maybe I can send Laszlo Vartek to help."

The thought of Vartek sent a rush of adrenalin though Doby. "I don't think we need him yet. I'll keep trying and let you know if I have any problems. Right now I have a computer hiccup that needs to be solved, and after that I'll devote everything to getting your information."

"I thank you so much for all your great efforts. You know how important it is."

"I understand."

Stefan von Portzer hung up.

Doby splashed himself another cup of coffee and headed back down to the computer room. Von Portzer was his major client, although he had a few others. Doby's talents were not the kind generally listed on a resume. He defined himself as a researcher, when in fact he was an expert in computer security, knowing how to work around firewalls and into databases. He didn't advertise his services, but a few clients had found him and he didn't need any others. They paid well, especially Stefan von Portzer.

His computer screen was stacked with a layer of popup ads. *Great.*

The one thing Doby didn't want at this point was for Laszlo Vartek to get involved. Vartek worked for von Portzer and was a research expert of another type. He knocked on doors and asked direct questions of people. And not so rarely, he ended up knocking on people. Vartek was one tough, gun-carrying character. No. It was better that von Portzer kept Vartek focused on other things.

... **Chapter 3** ...

Doby slid his chair toward his computer and began analyzing the intrusive software code. He tried to remember what he had been doing on the computer just before the problem occurred. He had visited various technical sites, looking for computer supplies, and he had tested a game on the Internet. He saved his other computer for sensitive research.

Playing games on the Internet wasn't his greatest interest, but computer games were often on the cutting edge of technology. And that could be an entertaining learning ground.

One game in particular caught his attention. It was called *Social Code*, and it was attracting more and more players. One online news site said it was the fastest growing game on the Internet. Just a few months before, only a few thousand people were playing the game, but now there were over a hundred thousand and the numbers were exponentially increasing each week. It cost each player ten US dollars a month to play.

Like many online games, players had to pass various levels, increasing in expertise. But a few things made Social Code unique. Yesterday, Doby had completed Level Two and then decided to quit.

One of the game's features was the choice of 'Professions'. The idea was to become a part of the 'Social Code Society' by choosing a certain Profession and then progressing from level to level within that Profession.

Currently the game had three Professions. The 'Arbitrator' role allowed a player to deal with civil code by acting as a judge or politician. The mind game.

'Citizen' was another mind game, but dealt with numerous cultural and social situations, and it also involved making investments, designing cities, and dealing with various kinds of personal relationships.

And then there was 'Protector', the action game. This was a typical blow-the-other-guy-apart game, full of exploding blood and guts.

The Social Code website informed users that more professions were being added shorly—one of these even now being tested with some players.

Doby learned that as players advanced from one level to the other, they had to enter a room and then answer various questions. These phases of the game were called 'The Test'. If the players successfully answered the questions, they advanced to the next level.

During the test, a computer-generated virtual character appeared and asked questions. Doby's character was a young woman named Lynette who wore a black robe and black headscarf at the first level.

The headscarf came off at Level Two.

Doby reached for his mouse, following an inkling of engineering intuition. The intrusive code . . . was it related to Social Code?

... # ...

Doby put his headset phone on, adjusting the speaker at the side of his mouth. He clicked the Social Code icon on his desktop, and the game's website appeared. The hourglass was no longer running. The Level Three Arbitrator game opened up and he picked up where he had left off. The computer sped up.

Of the three Professions currently available in Social Code, he had chosen to play the Arbitrator game. During the first two levels, he had acted as judge, watching court cases and then deciding whether the defendant was innocent or guilty. As in actual court cases, lawyers presented evidence and questioned witnesses, and a judge pronounced a verdict of guilty or innocent.

In the first two games he had judged the defendants not guilty. He had been correct.

On Level Three, Doby was to judge an armed robbery trial. The defendant was accused of robbing a bank, and his case ran for thirty minutes. With all the evidence and witness accounts—plus the testimony of the policemen who apprehended the robber outside the bank—Doby judged the defendant guilty.

Doby watched as 'Protector Policemen' led the accused to the middle of the digital courtroom where one of the policemen raised a sword and cut off the robber's hand. The people watching the case applauded.

A departure from the average execution of justice.

A door opened at the side of the court room and Doby moved through it.

Inside, he saw an image of the same woman who had appeared for the tests between previous levels. In her mid-twenties, she had wavy brunette hair that hung to her slim waist. But at this level, she was no longer dressed in her black headscarf and black robe. The current look was business professional—navy slacks and blazer and a white blouse—a low-cut blouse.

It was Lynette. The one who had acted as his guide during the test phases of the game.

"Hello, Mr. Gumbo," Lynette said, her computer-generated voice still managing to sound like American English. "You have been an admirable judge to make it here. Mr. Gumbo, are you ready to take the next challenge on your way toward becoming a Master Arbitrator?"

"Yes, Lynette," Doby answered. Gumbo was the alias he had given when he registered to play the game. He spoke through a program that altered his actual voice, changing the signal patterns in each word. He put great stock in anonymity.

"The test is considerable," Lynette continued. "As you did in previous levels, please move into the room on your right. We will begin when you are ready." She tilted her head, "Remember that you have a one-week deadline to complete the test. If you don't complete the test during that time, you will have to move back to Level Three and redo it."

Doby moved his mouse and directed his movement into the room. Once inside, he heard the door shut behind him. He moved to a table and Lynette materialized behind it. She bent over to take a piece of paper off the table, revealing cleavage where the top two buttons of her white blouse were undone.

Nice bit of programming, Doby thought.

... Chapter 4 ...

"Mr. Gumbo," Lynette said, "Are you ready to answer a set of questions?"

"Yes," Doby answered, wondering what algorithms they used in their voice recognition program.

"You are ready to move to Level Four. This means you will handle more difficult trials where discernment will become increasingly important. The world needs good judges. Does it not?"

"Yes." On most occasions, the game operated on players' yes-and-no answers. Still, Social Code's capabilities were exceptional, and it appeared that players could carry on rather complex dialogues with the game software—on its terms. But Doby had also discovered its limitations. "Does the world need good judges?" he asked.

"I ask the questions," Lynette replied.

"Yes," he said. Yes. It was limited.

Lynette smiled, "Then we will proceed with the test. Once completed, you can play Level Four. Your test requires filling in the following questionnaire."

A questionnaire appeared on the computer asking his shopping preferences, his yearly salary and his marital status. He gave false answers to all the questions.

It then asked for his name and address and he just typed in 'Dave Smith, New York Street, New York, New York."

Immediately Lynette came back on the screen, her eyes turned down and mouth frowning. "Mr. Gumbo, that is not your real name."

"Yes it is," Doby answered.

"If we send you money, then we need your real name."

"Why would you send me money?"

"Cash prizes," she answered.

"I don't need the money," he answered.

"Judges must be honest. They must give true information."

Doby wondered, what's going on here? Aloud, he said, "I need to pause."

"OK," Lynette answered. "See you soon." She smiled and bent over again to reach for papers—and to reveal more cleavage. Her image fragmented and disappeared but remained in Doby's mind as he wondered how they knew he had given a false name.

His credit card.

It cost ten dollars a month to subscribe to the game, and he paid this with a credit card. The name on his credit card was an alias name—John Burton. The credit card was linked to a Panama account under the name of John Burton. He used this for charging anything he bought over the Internet. Von Portzer had helped him setup up the account.

He went back to the website and entered the room. Lynette reappeared and said, "Welcome back Mr. Gumbo. Can you please complete the questionnaire?"

"Yes," Doby answered.

A summary of what he had already entered came up on the screen. The field with his name and address was still blank. He entered the name of John Burton and put in a fictitious address in New York. The questionnaire disappeared and Lynette reappeared.

"Thank you," she said. "You have successfully passed the test. Now you are invited to move to Level Four." She gestured with her arm at a door that materialized across the room.

Doby found himself looking at a virtual courtroom. Lynette stood inside, dressed in a black judge's robe.

"Hello Mr. Gumbo," she said.

"Yes," Doby replied.

"Welcome to Level Four. You are well on your way toward reaching expert level, but you have much learning in front of you. If you successfully pass Level Four, then you will take the first of a succession of special tests. Are you ready?"

"Yes," Doby replied, wondering what they meant by 'special tests'.

He moved to the judge's chair and watched a case unfold against a defendant charged with manslaughter.

After evaluating the evidence and testimonies, Doby pronounced the man guilty, remembering the sentencing of the last defendant. Immediately the Protector Policemen took the guilty man into the middle of the room, and with a long sword one of them chopped off the defendant's head. The other policemen picked up the head and held it in the air. Spectators in the courtroom applauded.

"Pretty brutal," Doby remarked aloud.

Lynette reappeared and said, "Justice is essential in a well functioning society. You have been an excellent judge and may now progress to the test that will take you to Level Five. Please enter the room on the right."

Doby moved into the room and Lynette appeared dressed in shorts and a tight t-shirt with Lara Croft proportions. She said, "Hello, Mr. Gumbo. You have been an admirable judge to make it here. Are you ready to take the test that will lead you to Level Five on your way toward becoming a Master Arbitrator?"

"Yes," Doby answered.

"Good," Lynette answered. "This test will be a little different than the others. You will meet with someone in person and be given a gift."

"Meet?" Doby questioned. "What do you mean?"

"I ask the questions," Lynette said.

"Yes."

"You will meet with someone in person and be given a gift. You need this gift to advance to other levels. It will come with instructions."

"Just send me the gift and instructions," Doby told the computer.

"Those are not the rules of the game. We provide personal attention in Social Code, and further rules of the game need to be explained by the person you meet."

Odd, but interesting. He shrugged his shoulders, "OK. Let's meet."

"Give a date, time and place," Lynette said.

At that, a form appeared on the screen, and Doby typed in Geneva's Buffet de la Gare at the central train station for eight o'clock that evening. He doubted it would register and was surprised when Lynette reappeared on the screen saying, "Thank you, Mr. Gumbo. Someone will be there at eight o'clock. He will be wearing black pants, black shoes, a long sleeved white shirt and a name badge that says 'Social Code' on it. He will be carrying a package, which is a present for you. Please be there, otherwise you will be penalized by being moved back to Level Three."

Lynette fragmented and disappeared.

... **Chapter 5** ...

"I have too much to do."

"Fred, I don't care. Just get it done." Bartholomew Strathmore looked Fred Hauser in the eyes. He needed to increase Fred's performance if the project was to advance. Bart had made exceptional progress—the number of players in the game was beyond his original projections, and the financials were even better than in the business plan.

But now he wanted to move faster. "We won't meet our financial targets unless you get it done," he said.

"Bart, I don't have time to get it done." Fred raised his hands in a show of defense, not surrender.

The two men sat across from each other at a small circular conference table, their bodies upright. Bart leaned forward, the expensive fabric of his business suit adjusting to the movement, "Do you want this project to be successful?"

"Sure, but there's only so much time in the day," Fred responded, shoving his glasses back up his nose for emphasis.

"So what's so hard about it?" Bart laid one hand on top of his other one, trying to present the epitome of calm.

Fred leaned back with a sigh, "It's not hard. It just takes time. What you are asking me to do is to access the PC of every player, copy their address books, and then market Social Code to all their contacts."

"Among other things." Bart had more important things to add to the game, but he wasn't ready to tell Fred quite yet. He needed to keep Fred focused, even though the man was already putting in sixteen to eighteen hours a day.

"Well, that takes a lot of time to set up the data bases," Fred explained. "Pulling the information off each player's computer is easy. It just takes time."

"Well, do it. It will increase our revenue streams and we need to maximize the game's financial potential." Bart paused. "And how is she coming?"

"She?"

"Pamela."

"She's slow."

"What do you mean?" Bart asked.

Fred shrugged and stretched his shoulder, pulling on the fabric of his Italian sports shirt. "I've been waiting to get more specifications from her, but she just sits there analyzing data."

"Well, what she's already done seems to be working, right?" Bart asked, knowing that the psychologist was responsible for the game's valuable logic in its test phases. Her work was a core feature in his business objectives. And she herself was a core feature for other objectives of his.

Fred was twisting a paper scrap into a rough origami bird, "Sure, the stickiness of players on the system is exceptional."

"And the sales are increasing, right?" Bart asked, linking his fingers together.

"Yeah, I'm amazed it's working so well," Fred formed a limp wing on the paper creature. "It's just that she gets carried away."

"With what?"

"She spends a lot of time analyzing the responses of individual players, getting sidetracked and wanting to provide them with therapy."

"We aren't here to help people," Bart stated with disdain. "We're here to make money and to build an organization."

"That isn't what she thinks," Fred said.

"I know. I had to negotiate to get her here. But it's working so far."

"Yeah." Fred was absorbed in folding a pointed beak.

Bart stood up and straightened his silk tie, "Then just keep her focused on the psych stuff. And stop her from getting sidetracked. The tests do need to be improved. Just make sure she doesn't see some of the other stuff we're doing."

"You have to talk to her, not me," Fred said, standing and looking at the lumpy bird he'd formed.

Bart started for the door, "I know. We just need to keep her productive."

Fred turned to follow, reaching for the paper bird and tossing it up in the air. It fell to the floor with no hint of flight.

... **Chapter 6** ...

Doby walked through the main hall of the Geneva train station, looking for someone wearing black pants and a white shirt and carrying a package.

He saw no one matching that description as he entered the Buffet de la Gare and found a table in the back corner. In keeping with his anonymity preferences, he had chosen to wear a NY baseball hat and a false goatee. He had switched his usual black-rimmed glasses for John-Lennon-like wire rims. He also wore a tweed jacket and a tie instead of his usual dark t-shirt and jeans.

Even his best friends wouldn't recognize him.

At exactly eight o'clock, a man entered the restaurant. Black pants, white shirt and a package. Doby rose in his chair, waved his arm and caught the man's attention. The man smiled and made his way across the room, dodging tables.

He approached Doby, stuck out his hand and said in French, "Hello. I'm glad you came Mr. Gumbo. My name is Runner."

Doby shook his hand, "Have a seat." Runner put the package on the table and sat in front of it. He seemed rather mesmerized by whatever was in the box. On Runner's shirt was pinned a black nametag that read, 'Mr. Runner, Protector, Social Code'. Doby guessed Runner to be between thirty-five and forty years old.

Runner stole a shy glance at Doby, shook himself a bit, and fumbled for a piece of paper from his shirt pocket. He cleared his throat and ducked his head to look at the page, "I have to read you this. It's part of the game."

"Go ahead," Doby said.

Runner swallowed, "The first thing it says is to welcome you to Level Five." He looked up at Doby as if to see that he had done this correctly.

"Thank you," Doby nodded with gentility.

Runner leaned forward in all earnestness, "If you have any questions, you just ask me."

"I will, thank you," Doby said, resisting the urge to smile. "Go ahead. Read your stuff."

"The second thing it says is that at Level Five you will be given more difficult tasks as you work your way to becoming a Master Arbitrator." Runner looked up from the paper and said with not a little touch of awe, "You become Master Arbitrator when you reach Level Ten."

"Master Arbitrator. What's that?" Doby could feel the goatee shifting with his frown.

Runner's eyes looked a bit glazed over, "They'll tell you as you move along. That's the fun of the game. It's like a mystery, but it becomes more interesting and you participate more, and," he lowered his voice in excitement, "they may even pay you real money."

Doby scratched his fake facial hair, "Participate more?"

"Yeah, but I can't say too much. I'm sworn to secrecy. You find out more when you reach Level Eight."

"So what did they tell you?"

"When I reached Level Eight Protector it got more interesting, but I really can't tell anything because I want to move from Level Nine to Level Ten Master Protector."

"Wow, Level Nine. That must have taken a lot of work," Doby

said, knowing that the first four levels had not taken any work at all.

"Getting to Level Nine meant working through a lot of segments," Runner said, lowering his chin in great seriousness. "And it has helped me."

"How's that?" Doby asked. He remembered Lynette mentioning segments.

"Look. You keep asking me questions I'm not allowed to answer. If I answer them, then I'll destroy everything for you. You have to enjoy the game and discover it on your own. With the gift here, the game starts to change for you. I can't say anything more because I absolutely have to reach Level Ten. I'm almost there. I failed the exam twice and hope to make it next time."

"Failed? How's that?"

Runner turned his eyes away from Doby and dropped his head for a moment. "Look, I have to read the list."

"Please read," Doby said.

"Three. You are now being given special tools to help you play the game. In the box are tools that will enable you to have a more rewarding playing experience. Please install and use them, otherwise you cannot continue to new levels. The operating instructions are inside."

"So what's in the box?" Doby asked.

Runner looked around and spoke softly. "Joysticks."

"Joysticks?" Doby asked.

"They're really cool," Runner said. "You use them to guide through the game."

"To what?"

"I'm only supposed to read through the list. The instructions are inside."

"OK. What else?" Doby asked.

"That's it."

"That's it?"

"Yeah. I read from the list and I gave you the free gift. If you use the joysticks, then you will progressively become a core member of the Social Code society."

Runner was holding the package. Doby noticed a faint sheen of sweat on his forehead. Doby looked at the package and waited. Runner carefully lifted it and handed it to Doby with both hands.

"These are very important."

"Thank you," Doby said. "Tell me, what do you do in real life?"

Runner blinked. "What do you mean?"

"Outside the game. Do you work here in Geneva?"

"I can't tell you."

"Why?"

"It's one of the basic rules of Social Code, secrecy. It is the right of each player to remain anonymous. So I shouldn't tell you what I do."

"Oh, come on. What can I do with that information? It's just between us as fellow Social Code players."

Runner bent forward. "I work in a factory—order fulfillment— but now Social Code is starting to pay me something every time I distribute the joysticks. And at Level Ten I can make more, maybe even work for Social Code. Then I could leave the factory."

"Where do they get the money to pay you?"

Runner looked dumbfounded. "I don't know. All I know is that they ship me a few boxes with joysticks and every once in a while they send me instructions and I give one away, like tonight. Then as soon as you play with them, they know to pay me and send the money directly to my bank account. Someone told me that at Level Ten they pay you more and maybe even hire you."

"Sounds interesting. Full time employment."

"It's more than that."

"Like what?"

Runner looked Doby in the eyes. "Social Code is spectacular. Look. You have to find out for yourself. If I say more it's like telling you the end of an exciting movie." Runner looked across at the package sitting on Doby's side of the table. "I did my job. Now I have to go."

Doby lifted a hand, "Could I ask one last question?"

"Sure." Runner gave an unsure half-smile.

"Who runs the game?"

The smile turned to a frown. "It's a secret. I already told you. Anonymity is one of the rules of Social Code. We all have pseudonyms and our identities are protected, including the people running the game, the Forming Team."

"The Forming Team?" Doby asked.

"That's what all the other players are calling them."

"How do you know it's a team?" Doby asked.

"I don't know," Runner began rubbing his hands then scratched his face. "I never asked those kinds of questions. I heard about someone starting the game. A guy I know from Boston told me that he thinks the game's founder is from Boston. Anyway, there have to be several people to do something so brilliant, don't you think?

That's all I know." Runner stood up. "Look. I gotta go."

Doby stood as well, package in one hand. He extended the other to Runner, "OK, thanks for your help and for the gift."

"It's cool. Use it well." Runner's handshake was damp. He left the room and Doby held the package out in front of him. Just a box wrapped in plain brown paper with a label.

Doby headed out of the restaurant and left the station in the direction of his parked motorcycle. As he checked for traffic, he saw a small, older model Citroen exit the underground parking to stop at a red light. Runner was driving the car, his eyes focused on the street in front of him, his face a blank plate behind the wheel.

When the light turned green the Citroen did not move. Only when a horn honked behind the Citroen did Runner snap his head and accelerate.

Doby took a pen from his pants' pocket and jotted down the Citroen's license number on the package. He managed to get down all the digits just as the car disappeared around the corner.

The expressionless look on Runner's face made Doby uneasy.

... Chapter 7 ...

"Welcome Mr. Pitbill. You have now reached Level Ten, the highest level of Social Code. You are a valiant warrior."

"Thank you Angelica," Pitbill said. She looked more beautiful than ever, so young and innocent. How he admired her flowing blond hair and ivory skin, and today her clothing was almost transparent. He tried to focus on her words and not her very visible breasts.

"Now you are a Master Protector. Very few have made it to this level. Are you willing to assume all the responsibilities required of you?"

"Yes."

"Then I shall explain them to you. First, the rules of Social Code are good."

"I shall follow the rules of Social Code," Pitbill responded.

"I trust you," Angelica stated. "Secondly, you shall play Social Code every day. There is an action segment and a self-awareness segment. Are you willing to do this?"

"Yes."

"Third, as a Master Protector, you will be called upon to protect the players of Social Code, to enact justice, and to work together as decided by Master Arbitrators. Just as you distributed joysticks to players during your initiation, now you take on a more important role within our society. Are you willing to do this?"

"Yes."

"Do you have a gun, a real gun?"

"Yes."

"That's good. Soldiers and policemen—protectors of society and justice need weapons to effectively do their work. That's what you are now, a real protector of society and justice. From time to time you may need your gun."

"Yes."

"That's excellent. From time to time I will call upon you to assist Master Arbitrators and thereby to carry out your calling as a Master Protector. Are you willing to do this?"

"Yes."

"As a Master Protector, Social Code will now make some payments to you, a small stipend on a regular monthly basis, but significantly more whenever you carry out an act of protection on behalf of Social Code. Do you accept?"

"Yes."

"Mr. Pitbill, I can only say that you have attained a privileged and honorable position within the Social Code society. You are a great and honorable man. Are you willing to always carry out my wishes?"

"Yes."

"Thank you Mr. Pitbill. And, there is one last thing I want to say."

"Yes." He barely formed the word, his lips were so dry.

The fine transparent cloth dropped to her waist and her hips shifted. "Pitbill, I love you."

"I love you too, Angelica."

... # ...

Doby unwrapped the package and pulled out the joysticks,

tossing the wrappings into the trash near his television. He noticed on the TV that the stock markets were moving up, and he regretted that he did not have time to make an investment.

He turned back to the Social Code gift. Two joysticks attached to a flat rectangular plastic base. One was stationary, fixed perpendicularly to the plastic base. The other joystick could be rotated from the base and its top was covered with buttons like most standard joysticks. Under the plastic base, suction cups could attach the device to a table. A cable extended from the back with a USB plug at its end.

What made the two joysticks unique was their metal handles, similar to handles on a exercise cross-trainer for monitoring the user's heart rate.

A CD-ROM and instruction book accompanied the device. The first step was to load the software from the CD-ROM, so Doby inserted it into the disc in his drive and did so. When the software was loaded he stuck the USB plug in the slot into his computer.

He put his hands on the joysticks, and immediately his computer opened up to the Social Code website.

Lynette appeared. "Hello Mr. Gumbo. I see you have successfully installed your gift." Her body swayed seductively back and forth. She was wearing a tight white t-shirt.

"Yes," Doby said. "Now what?"

"I would like to ask you some questions, just to see that the joysticks are properly working."

"Yes."

"How do you feel?" Lynette asked.

"OK."

"I think you feel more than OK," Lynette stated.

"What do you mean?"

"You are slightly nervous."

"Why should I be nervous?" Doby looked down at the joysticks he was holding. Was the computer program monitoring his heartbeat? "Yeah, maybe," he said.

"Don't worry. We will work on this. I will help you learn to control your emotions, if you let me."

"I would like that," Doby said wondering what the response of the computer driven image would be.

"Me too," Lynette said. "Please trust me. This will be fun."

"OK."

"You feel nervous."

"Yes."

"Now you are telling the truth."

"How do you know that?" Doby asked.

Lynette shifted back and forth. She wasn't wearing a bra. "I ask the questions."

"How old are you?" Doby asked.

"I ask the questions." Lynette stated. She shifted exactly as before.

"OK." Doby said.

"We will start with a little game," Lynette said.

"I'm ready," Doby said.

"I want to test your ability to concentrate and relax at the same time. Look into my face and hold the joysticks. You don't need to move them. I will sense when you are ready and then I will ask you questions. This may take some time."

"I'm ready."

Lynette's face came closer to the screen. Doby noticed that it was perfectly generated with ivory white skin and unusually light blue-gray eyes. He held the joysticks and looked into her face.

After five minutes Lynette softly said, "I sense you need to relax more, Mr. Gumbo."

"How do you know?" He looked down at his hands on the sticks.

"I ask the questions."

"Yes." He stifled a yawn. This was getting boring.

"Please don't talk. You will destroy the effect of the game. I want you to relax," she said with a soft voice.

Despite himself, Doby relaxed.

"That's better," Lynette quietly said, her face inching closer. "Now relax some more."

Doby noticed that Lynette's eyes had grown slightly larger. His own eyes felt heavy.

"Let your legs relax," she crooned.

Doby let his legs relax.

"That's good, now let your chest, stomach and back relax."

Doby felt his torso go heavy and light at the same time.

"Now let your shoulders and arms relax...and your neck." Lynette's eyes became large blue pools.

"You are relaxing very nicely." Lynette tilted her head, "I like it."

Doby felt himself drifting off to the sound of Lynette's voice which had grown lower and slower.

"I want the best for you Mr. Gumbo. I want to be your friend. You must come back often to play with me, to play Social Code. Now, tell me Mr. Gumbo, will you come back to play with me?"

"Yes," Doby said.

"I like that. Will I see you today or tomorrow?"

"Yes," Doby answered. He faintly realized the computer program did not pick up on his imprecise answer. Another weakness in their system.

"Excellent," Lynette told him. "That is enough for now. Why don't you go lie down and shut your eyes a little bit, maybe even go to sleep. Think of me and how I want the best for you. I want to get to know you."

Soft music emanated from his computer's speakers.

Doby wanted to see where the game was going. Why not take a cat nap? He went over to the small cot and laid down. He shut his eyes and fell asleep.

... **Chapter 8** ...

Doby blinked at the clock. How was it morning already? He didn't remember lying down, but he had probably needed the sleep after several late nights working on the von Portzer project.

He looked over at his problematic computer and saw the two joysticks. Then he remembered. Lynette. He had been having a discussion with her.

Though he felt compelled to return to the joysticks and enter the game, he refrained from doing so.

Actually, the game wasn't very challenging, but it had kept him engaged from level to level. It even appeared to have drawn him into a relaxation exercise. And now, he felt a deep desire to go back and play the game. He resisted the temptation.

Rising from his cot, he walked over to the joysticks and examined them closely. He unplugged the joystick's cable from the USB port and plugged it into his other computer. From a cupboard, he pulled out a small oscilloscope for measuring electrical currents. He attached the oscilloscope to his PC.

But when he placed his hands on the joysticks, nothing happened. Maybe they need the software? He loaded the CD-ROM into the auxiliary computer. The installation program began to run but then stopped and asked him to go online. That would take him to the Social Code Internet site, so it looked like the computer program needed a handshake.

He would have to crack the code and disable this. Just his kind of thing.

For the next four hours he worked on the CD-ROM code, managing to break the link to the Internet. After several attempts to load the Social Code software, he finally did it. Now he was able to run the joysticks without being connected to the Internet.

When he held the joysticks again, the oscilloscope dial jumped. The joysticks were picking up a signal—several signals, in fact.

He let go and snapped his fingers. The joysticks were some form of a polygraph, a lie detector. That is how Lynette was able to say he was nervous.

For the next two hours, he researched lie detectors online, clicking through several technical websites to figure out how they worked and the types of signals they generated in various circumstances. Some voice-generated lie detectors measured stress and anxiety in the voice. It looked like Social Code was using a combination of signals from the joysticks and his voice as a means of monitoring physiological reactions.

He spent the afternoon writing a computer program that emulated the joystick and voice stress signals. He loaded the program into his handheld PDA, and with his stylus he could move a button up or down to increase or decrease his stress level.

After practicing different emotions and responses, he looked at his watch and realized he had not worked on von Portzer's research. He ran upstairs, grabbed a yogurt and opened the files on the German businessman.

He would have to wait till tomorrow to test the device.

... # ...

Lynette wore a low cut halter-top revealing some serious cleavage.

"Good morning Mr. Gumbo. I hope you slept well."

"Yes," Doby answered.

"Are you ready to play with me again?"

"Yes."

"Did you enjoy playing last time?" She asked.

"Did you enjoy playing last time?" Doby asked, testing the system.

"I ask the questions," she stated, swaying back and forth.

"OK," Doby replied.

"Did you enjoy playing last time?" She asked again.

"Yes."

"Now, I would like to get to know you, to help you to learn to relax. May I ask you some questions?."

"Yes."

"How are you feeling?" Lynette asked.

"OK," Doby stated.

"You seem to be slightly nervous."

"I guess." On his PDA, Doby moved the button upward. The electronic signal flew up and down in a given range. He moved it up even more.

"You seem to be nervous," she said.

So his program was working. His PDA was plugged into a USB port next to where the joysticks were plugged in. He had a long cable attached from the computer to the PDA, enough for him to make his way around the room. In his chair he swiveled over to his auxiliary computer that was now recording Lynette. Everything appeared to be operating correctly.

"Yes," he remembered to say.

"I can help you relax, to reach a clear state where you are freed from the aberrations of the mind."

"OK."

"As you did last time, just stare into my eyes and relax. This may take several minutes."

Lynette's face filled the computer screen.

After a minute Doby moved the button on the PDA down followed by the heart rate button.

"Good, keep relaxing," she said, her eyes enlarging ever so slightly.

A minute later he moved the buttons down again.

"You learn quickly." Lynette's voice was slower and lower. "Now, let your body become relaxed . . . you feel tired."

Doby moved the buttons down further.

"Do you like this game Mr. Gumbo?"

"Yes."

"I will now ask you some questions."

"Yes."

"Do you enjoy Social Code?"

"Yes."

"How old are you?"

"Twenty nine." Doby gave his actual age.

"What is your occupation?"

"Factory worker, now and then."

"Do you like your occupation?"

"No."

"Are you married?"

"Almost, once." Doby smiled. He had never been married and his last girl friend had left him six months before. She told him he spent too much time married to his silly computers.

"Are you lonely?"

"Yes, sometimes." At least he had answered correctly on that one.

"Do you like female company?"

"Yes."

"What is your income?"

Thirty thousand dollars per year." Lie again. It was much more, but Lynette didn't need to know that."

"I thank you for your honesty," Lynette stated. "I know you were honest with me."

"Yes," he said. Lynette's program was reading the signals generated by his PDA and not those coming from his hands on the joysticks. He could now adjust the stress level to whatever he wanted.

"And you are a fast learner. I can teach you to relax." She continued.

"Yes."

"And to gain control of yourself, to be worthy."

"Yes."

"I can help you."

"Yes."

"We can have fun together playing Social Code."

"Yes. Can I play with you?" he asked.

"I ask the questions."

"OK," he replied. "We can have fun together playing Social Code."

"You will want to become an inside member of the Social Code Society."

"Yes."

"You will want to play the game, learn the Social Code ethics, and follow the covenants."

"Yes."

"Now, you may want to shut your eyes and relax and even go lie down for a while. The test is finished. When you are ready you can advance to Level Five. Congratulations." She lowered her voice, "I want you to come back soon."

Soft music began to play as Lynette's image disappeared. Swirling blue and white clouds appeared on the screen, pulsing in time with the music.

... Chapter 9 ...

Odd. Doby replayed the interaction with Lynette and then went onto the other computer and typed 'hypnosis' into a search engine. For the next half hour he read several articles on the topic.

Social Code's structure had all the tell-tale signs of hypnosis. The game used autosuggestion techniques, but for what end? That interested him, but not as much as how the game's software was technically constructed. And most importantly, how had it invaded his computer files?

Neither had he forgotten those popup ads that kept appearing whenever he wasn't playing Social Code.

He scanned the computer and found more foreign code than before imbedded in the operating system. Additional code was also lurking in the Internet browser. It had the look and feel of spyware. Rather than removing it, he decided to let it run.

If it was spyware, he was curious how they would spy on him and how they would use that information. To find out, he did some random searching, visiting fishing and hunting sites and one site for Russian brides. For the fun of it, he checked out several travel sites, particularly cheap package deals to the Caribbean islands.

Doby then copied the Social Code software and loaded it on the auxiliary computer in a secure environment.

"Let's see what happens now," he said to his monitor.

... # ...

Pitbill waited all day to enter Social Code. First he practiced with the action game, perfecting his skills and timing. He still stalked through streets, blasting away at the bad guys. But now the bad guys could be anybody. In fact, the characters in the game were no longer monsters, but normal-looking people, which made the game more challenging. He was obliged to take out anyone with a gun in their hand. And anyone could be carrying a gun—men, women and children. The trick was shooting before he was shot.

At this level, the bad people sometimes received a court sentence, and then they were let lose on the streets. If the game said, 'I command you to shoot,' then the task of the Master Protector was to carry out justice, no matter if the command was to shoot an adult or a child. Those were the rules.

For Pitbill, the Level Ten Protector action was the ultimate challenge.

Even better were the blissful times as Angelica led him through relaxation exercises. She was sensitive to all his emotions and feelings. With her, he did not have to think rationally or logically. She knew him so well and was helping him gain confidence in himself, to clear his aberrations and master his self-awareness.

Angelica continually instructed Pitbill to actualize the game into all his life, bringing the covenant into every facet of his existence. And yesterday she had told him he would soon have the opportunity to bring the authority of Social Code into the world around him. The world would be a better place when this happened. He would be called upon to act as a true Master Protector. The Social Code Society needed him.

... # ...

Doby scratched his jaw—he'd skipped shaving the last two days. They were loading new code into his system.

Comparing the computer files from one day to the next, he had found the new code—and found that some old code was being removed. This happened when a player moved from one level to the next. In fact, it took place in the exact moment a player moved into the virtual room to take the tests between each level.

This new code was being supplied from a central server somewhere, and the whole structure was a very clever construction.

Not only that, as the player advanced from level to level, Social Code was in effect taking over the player's PC, and when the PC was online, Social Code was monitoring the player more and more.

Doby put his feet up on his desk and sat back in amazement. This was an extremely sophisticated software environment and it meant that world class technical people were behind it.

They weren't just invading the PC. Monitoring stress levels and implementing hypnotic techniques meant the game was out to influence players. Influence them how . . . and how far would they go?

... **Chapter 10** ...

When Doby downloaded Gumbo's email, he saw sixteen new messages in his in-box. Some were ads for fishing poles, hooks, super lures, fishing boats and electronic fish spotting radar. One message offered a fifty-percent discount off hunting boots and jackets. Another featured a recent batch of email-order brides from Eastern Europe.

No mistake—these messages were directly targeted to John Burton, alias Gumbo. Spyware was certainly at work, and someone was building a personal portfolio of John Burton.

One message puzzled Doby. Its subject read 'Thank You For Your Order'. Order? He clicked it open to find an order confirmation and a password to access a website for one year. He clicked on the website address. It directed him to the website 'Artistic Photos: Thousands of Thumbnails of Teenage Girls Doing Nasty Things.'

"What on earth?" he asked aloud. "I never placed an order for this." He had already guessed that Social Code must be getting a percentage of the sales generated from targeted marketing, but this one was a confirmation of an order. It must be a gimmick. He didn't bother typing in the password but closed the site's page and went back to Gumbo's email.

The last message was from Lynette. He opened it.

Dear Mr. Gumbo,

I personally want to congratulate you on reaching Level 5 in Social

Code. At Level 5 you are entering an elite membership. Social Code is becoming one of the top games on the Internet and I am happy to get to know you. Remember that Social Code is more than a game. It is a chance to learn, grow, and become part of a worldwide society.

I look forward to getting to know you better as we advance through the game together.

My warm regards,
Lynette

As soon as he closed the message, new ads popped up. The first was a one-time offer for Jim Bowie hunting knives, another for Russian brides and a third for discount trips to the Caribbean for singles.

He slammed his fist near his keyboard. Who are these people? He took a deep breath and realized he had a couple of alternatives.

One was just to stop playing the game and finish the research for Stefan von Portzer. The other was to find out who this so-called founding team was and whether he could outsmart them. It was the challenge of the second alternative that motivated him the most. Curiosity mixed with anger makes for an odd motivation.

There was also a realization that further development on his website would be delayed. He had chosen to name it after himself, in a round about way, and wanted to use the site to test some advanced functionality. But, now the game was filling his mind and there was no time.

How to find them? He considered one way. There would be a record of his payment of Social Code's ten-dollar monthly subscription.

Online, he accessed his bank in Panama and looked at his account. The payments to Social Code were going into a bank in the Cayman Islands. Probably an offshore company owned the account, and it would be virtually impossible to determine their identity. He made note of the bank. Accessing the records of banks was difficult, but not impossible, and he did have some experience.

Then he took a look at his balance. He almost fell out of his chair. Zero. The balance was zero.

... # ...

Bart banged the door shut behind him and strode into the room. Without saying hello, he asked, "Did you get it?"

Fred looked up from his computer screen, startled. "Get what?"

"The offshore account."

Fred made a face. "I don't know why we're doing this. We're already making enough money from the game and the marketing."

Bart glared back, "You don't need to know why we're doing this, other than it's important. Did you get the money?"

"Yeah, sure, a simple billing, but he knows where the payment was made."

"Don't worry about it," Bart said. "A shell company holds that account, and I doubt he'll ever pursue it. You said he lives in Switzerland, right?"

Fred nodded.

Bart sat down in his chair and swung his feet up on his desk. His trouser cuffs slid back to reveal silk argyle socks. "Most people make their payments from banks in their home countries. Why would he be paying from a Panama bank, unless its a discrete little stash he doesn't want anyone to know about? And who's he going to tell about buying time on a porn site?"

"But why deplete his account?" Fred asked.

"You said he's a good player, right?" Bart had asked Fred to perform a statistical analysis on players, to see who gave the most correct answers and advanced most rapidly through the different levels.

"He's in the top percentile."

It was Bart's turn to nod. "And we don't have many Level Ten people in Europe yet, do we?" Bart swung his feet to the floor and stood up.

"No," Fred answered, knowing the conversation was over.

Bart walked to the door. "Think about market expansion. Put a little pressure on the guy and monitor his reactions." Bart shut the door hard behind him.

... **Chapter 11** ...

Doby stood up so fast, his chair went spinning and bounced off the other table. A few days ago he had thirty thousand dollars in that account—a payment received from Stefan von Portzer.

He somehow knew but checked anyway. The money had been transferred to a bank in the Bahamas. He read 'Payment for artistic photos', and almost sat down without the chair underneath him.

Poof. Thirty thousand dollars gone, just like that. Doby had worked hard for that money. Many long days and late nights and pots of coffee working for von Portzer. Sure, he had more money than that in his Swiss bank account, but this was more about principal than anything else.

Thirty thousand dollars for a year's access to a porn site.

He retrieved his chair, slumped down into it and closed his eyes. After gathering himself together, he opened them and surveyed the room as if it would offer some solution. Several stacks of paper were on the verge of toppling, the floor needed to see a broom, and the muted TV on the wall was advertising a new car model. And next to his ill computer sat the harmless-looking joysticks on their plastic stand.

He put on his headset, thumped his mouse on its pad and clicked onto the Social Code website.

Lynette appeared. She was wearing a t-shirt. A tiny t-shirt. "Hello Mr. Gumbo. I was waiting for you."

"I was too busy," Doby said.

"You said you would get back to me."

"I'm so sorry."

"I forgive you. But now that you are an elite member of Social Code, you must think about your commitments."

"My commitments. What do you mean?"

"I ask the questions," Lynette said.

"OK."

"Do you want to play the game?"

"Yes."

"You are now at Level Five."

"I want to change from Judge to Protector."

"Are you sure?"

"Yes. very sure."

"Then please wait a minute while I make the changes."

Lynette disappeared and his computer light started blinking. They were loading software onto his computer. Two minutes later Lynette reappeared.

"You are now ready to change to Protector," Lynette stated. "It may take you some time to learn the game and gain skills, so please don't become frustrated. You can pause at any time. The object is to eliminate the enemy and find the goal that will take you to Level Six."

"The goal?"

"The goal is a door. When you find the door you will enter a room to take the test. I will meet you there. Are you ready to play?"

"Yes."

The screen changed and immediately he found himself in a maze of rooms. A handgun protruded from the center of the screen's game space. He was unable to move the handgun in any direction and quickly calculated that he needed to use the joysticks to move around.

He did not like the idea of that. There must be a technical substitution he could find. Just touching the joysticks made him feel creepy.

Lynette appeared. "Are you using the joysticks?" she asked.
"No."

"You must use the joysticks. After Level Five, the entire game is played with the joysticks."

"OK," he said.

He sighed and grabbed the joysticks. Perhaps he could write a code to run simulated joysticks from his PDA, like he had done for the lie detector. For the moment he decided to use the joysticks for the action segments of the game, reverting to his invented electronic device when it came to tests.

Doby fired away at ugly monsters, blowing them apart. He was happily imagining them to be the programmers responsible for his thirty grand when he had an idea.

If the software for the action part of the game was sitting on his computer, then he might be able to analyze it and program a player to play the game. Then he wouldn't have to touch the joysticks or even mess around with a stylus on a PDA, and he could just walk away from the game and let his virtual player do his thing. Pausing the game, he went over to the auxiliary computer with the Social Code software and began looking into the code.

Five hours, three cups of coffee, and a protein bar later he had created an electronic player. John Burton was now a computer program playing against Social Code, mano a mano, program against program. To the code he also added the stress monitor from his PDA. Burton's stress level would match the game's action.

Whenever the enemy appeared, John Burton would blast it away and his adrenaline would be pumping.

And the best thing was that John Burton knew every move of the enemy.

Doby loaded the John Burton software on the Social Code computer and John took over, shooting every enemy and sending his 'personal' signals through the heart rate monitor and lie detector. Doby sat back and smiled.

Within thirty minutes John Burton had destroyed hundreds of enemies and was standing in front of the goal door to take the next test.

Then Doby frowned and leaned forward. Had he made John Burton too perfect? John never made a mistake or wasted a shot. He knew where every monster was hiding and sought them out with the greatest of efficiency. What if the designers of Social Code noticed that?

Doby switched off the John Burton software, put his hand on the arrow keys, adjusted the stress monitor program on his PDA and warily moved inside the door to face Lynette and take the test.

... **Chapter 12** ...

Doby just wanted to get to the higher levels as soon as possible. Runner had mentioned that Social Code made payments to some players. Maybe he could find out more about the founders if he made it to Level Ten.

He was also curious to see what kind of new software they would be loading on his computer at each new level. And while the alien code on the PC and incessant popup adds still antagonized him, it was the Panama bank transaction that made him furious.

Sure, he could just unplug from Social Code, swallow his losses, and walk away from the whole thing.

But he wasn't going to.

He moved Gumbo into the room and Lynette appeared.

"Congratulations, Mr. Gumbo. You have successfully completed the action game of Level Six. Would you like to take the test to move to Level Seven?" Lynette's halter top did not seem to be covering much.

Doby felt like telling Lynette he liked that little nothing she was almost wearing. But he didn't—instead, he just replied with his required, "Yes," not wanting to slow down the game.

Lynette smiled and said, "If you want to take the test, please go through the door on the right."

Doby moved through the door. Social Code was changing software on his PC. Some of the code from the Level Five game was being removed and the Level Six code was being added. At the same time, more adware and spyware was oozing its way into the files on his computer. This made his skin itch, but he did nothing about it. Once Social Code finished loading the software, he would make a copy, move it to his auxiliary PC, analyze it, and prepare John Burton's strategy for the next action game.

He entered the next room and found Lynette there.

"Mr. Gumbo," she said, "This is to let you know that the test for Level Six Protector will enable you to rise to greater heights. The test is complex and will require your entire concentration. Our objective is to help clear your mind from unwanted sensations and emotions, irrational fears and psychosomatic illnesses. It starts with an audit of your subconscious mind. You will gain greater control over your being, a new level of awareness. Is this what you want?"

"Yes," he said, thinking, I want my money back.

"Do you want to become a master of your own destiny?"

"Yes." Whose destiny?

"Do you want to participate in a new society, one without insanity, without unlawfulness and without conflict, where you can prosper and exercise your rights?

"Yes." *Blah, blah*, he thought.

"Do you want to follow the covenants of the Social Code Society?"

"Yes." He leaned over to his auxiliary computer and recorded his voice saying 'yes' and 'no' then wrote a small program that would automatically answer yes or no by typing 'Y' or 'N' keyboard. He moved the program back to the machine running Social Code and tested it. It worked.

Still, he was forced to listen to the test, and he wished he could design some software to automatically take the test for him, just like the John Burton software that played the action games. The problem was, he didn't have the tests on his PC. They were running on a central server somewhere.

He resigned himself to keep listening and typing 'Y' or 'N' while Lynette led him through a series of relaxation exercises. He tried to ignore her, but listening to her voice made him feel tired and he began to drift into her soft melodic voice.

After several minutes, Doby's eyelids closed of their own will, his head falling back against his chair.

... # ...

Somewhere in the background, Lynette was repeating a question.

"Mr. Gumbo, can you answer me?"

"Huh?" he said, opening his eyes and blinking at Lynette's face on the computer.

"Mr. Gumbo, can you answer my question?"

He must have fallen asleep in his chair. "Yes," he mumbled.

"Mr. Gumbo, can you answer my question?"

He had forgotten that he had to push the 'Y' key on his keyboard. He pushed it.

"Thank you," Lynette replied.

"Now, I want you to stay deeply relaxed and listen to my voice. You are very relaxed," Lynette said. "There are things you like to buy."

"Yes."

"You like vacations to the Caribbean."

"Yes."

"You like hunting and fishing," Lynette softly affirmed.

"Yes."

"You like Russian brides and photos of girls," She said.

Doby stiffened, hesitated and then hit 'Y.' Yeah, like thirty thousand dollars worth of photos, he thought.

... **Chapter 13** ...

When the test ended, Doby advanced to the Level Seven Protector action game.

Some test, he thought. It was just a big marketing scam. They moved players quickly to Level Five and gave them the joysticks. Then with the joysticks they could monitor the emotions of the player and use hypnosis and repetitive conditioning to make the person more susceptible to suggestion. And then they sold them products. But why the photos?

It dawned on him. There was no inventory. Other products meant shipping merchandise, possible returns, expenses. With digital photos there was none of that, pure revenue. Very clever scheme.

Still, he wondered at Social Code's audacity to charge him thirty thousand dollars. If they did that to everyone, players would be flooding the credit card companies to get their money back, and Social Code would lose all its players. They appeared to have singled him out.

Who were they? He knew practically nothing about the people behind Social Code.

He reached for a piece of paper and scribbled 'Founding team, how many?; sophisticated programmers, beyond typical Internet games; relaxation and hypnosis techniques; money making enterprise; why me?'

And off paper he wondered, did they create the game only to make money, or did some further motive lie behind the whole enterprise?

While he should be spending time on the von Portzer project, he wanted to advance through the higher levels and see if he could come any closer to the humans behind this.

Doby clicked on the Social Code icon. Immediately Lynette appeared and said, "Welcome Mr. Gumbo. Congratulations. You have reached Level Seven." Doby barely noted her partially transparent ensemble as she asked, "Are you ready to play?"

"Yes," Doby pushed the 'Y' key.

"Then begin," she commanded.

A hand with a gun appeared, so Doby hit the F12 key where the John Burton software was waiting, ready to play. Within two seconds there was a blast as John Burton blew a creature-man in half.

Doby went upstairs for a sandwich.

... # ...

Descending the stairs with a stack of sliced salami, cheese, and tomatoes between thick slabs of farmer's bread, Doby glanced at the computer monitor. John Burton was still making most of his shots and racking up points.

Doby turned to his auxiliary computer and went online. How had Runner known about the Founding Team of Social Code?

Runner said he worked at a factory. Geneva was home to many factories, and Doby wished he had asked Runner more personal questions. Then he remembered—he had jotted down Runner's license plate number on the joystick packaging.

Doby took a bite from his sandwich and bent down to look in his waste paper baskets. They were full to the brim. Luckily he hadn't emptied them in quite a while, but he couldn't remember exactly where he had put the brown paper wrapping. He dug through two of them, chewing on the coarse salami and cursing himself for not entering the license number in his PDA.

He was relieved to find the wrapping crumpled up in the third trash bin. He straightened the brown paper to find Runner's license number. He went to his auxiliary computer and got online. Using some special backdoor software, he went directly to the database of the Service des Automobiles for the Canton of Geneva.

He had been there before. Doby knew his way around all of the state databases in Geneva and also the federal databases in Bern.

Occasionally Stefan von Portzer asked him to do research on Swiss residents. Geneva was a city full of international organizations and multinational companies, and Stefan often needed confidential information on people for business transactions. He paid Doby to access their taxes and police records and even to find out what cars they owned.

Doby entered the database, and in a few seconds he found a match. And 'Runner's' name and address. His name was Pierre Bailloud and he lived on the Route de Vernier in Geneva.

Doby then accessed the database of the Social Security department of Geneva and found out where Pierre Bailloud worked. It was for a company called TimeSync. Further research revealed that TimeSync supplied parts for companies in the watch-making industry. Their factory employed forty-five people and was located in an industrial zone in the southern part of Geneva.

Most factory work days in Geneva ended at five o'clock. Doby put his computers on suspend and jogged upstairs. He rummaged around for the false goatee and Lennon glasses. Grabbing the tweed jacket on his way out the door, he pulled out his motorcycle and drove down through the farm hills toward the factory site. Once there, he stopped across the street from the factory parking lot and waited.

Shortly after five o'clock, a mass of people left the building. Just when he thought he had missed him, Doby spotted Runner walking alone, head down and lost in thought. Runner went to his car, the small Citroen.

Doby followed the Citroen on his motorcycle for several kilometers until it came to Route du Vernier. Runner parked and got out.

Doby drove his motorcycle up to Runner and said casually, "Hey, how are you doing?"

Runner furrowed his brow and asked, "Do I know you?"

"Sure," Doby answered, taking off his crash helmet. "You're Runner. My name is Gumbo. We met at the train station. I thought I recognized you driving by in your car. How's the game going?"

Runner looked cautiously in both directions and said, "I'm not supposed to talk to the people I give joysticks to. That's part of the rules. I could get negative points for this." He rubbed his hands on his sides and shifted his weight.

"Don't worry," Doby said, holding out a hand, "I won't tell anyone."

"You sure?" Runner looked relieved.

"Yeah. It's just a game anyway."

"It's more than a game," Runner said, expressing fierce belief.

Doby lowered his voice, looking Runner in the eye. "You're right. It's more than a game. Tell me, did you reach Level Ten?"

Runner blushed. "No. I have failed four times now, but each time

I'm getting closer."

"Failed the test. Why?" Doby set his helmet in his lap and adjusted his balance on the bike.

"Each level becomes harder and longer. The one I'm now on takes a lot of concentration, to make sure I respond properly."

"Respond to what?" Doby asked.

Runner looked both ways again. "You have the joysticks now, so I guess I can tell you. It takes a lot of concentration and relaxation. But it's really wonderful. After making an audit of your subconscious state, the game guides you through a set of responses. It actually helps you redesign your inner state. You can reach a new level of awareness and confidence."

"No kidding." Doby was having a hard time not sounding sarcastic.

"What level are you at?" Runner asked.

"Just moved to Level Six."

"That's good. A Level Six Judge."

"No, like you said, I was able to switch. I'm now going for Level Six Protector."

Runner smiled. "Then you have a ways to go to get to where I'm at. It takes a lot of skill."

"I know. I admire you," Doby stated. "I'll just keep trying." Doby paused, hesitated and said, "There is one thing you said at the train station I have been wondering about."

"What's that?"

"You said the people behind the game must be brilliant to create something so spectacular. How did you found out about them? You mentioned a guy you knew."

"By chance. I found out through a buyer from Boston who came to my factory looking for watch pieces. We had lunch together and I found out he is a player. He said the founders come from his city." Doby hoped he wouldn't frighten Runner into silence, but he asked anyway, "How does he know?"

Runner had a quizzical look on his face. "I don't know. I didn't ask him . . . anyway, one of the game's covenants is individual privacy."

Doby placated him, "I know, I know. We have to respect the rules, but this guy, your friend from Boston, knew something. And you actually met him." Doby hoped he was making Runner feel he was the owner of exceptional information. Information he would want to show off. "Do they have watch factories in Boston?"

"No, this guy's company is a reseller, Distru-Ware. They stock parts and resell them to companies in the U.S. They buy a lot from us."

"No kidding," Doby said. "So, what's his name?"

"Who?" Runner asked.

"The guy from the reseller. Distru-Ware. What's his name?"

"I'm not supposed to give information about other players."

"Let's not call him a player then," Doby suggested. "Let's just call him a guy from Distru-Ware. Maybe I need a good contact in the US to help with distribution."

Runner looked up and down the street then whispered, "His name is William Marder."

"That's cool," Doby said, lowering his voice, "You met a guy who might even know the founders."

"Only one of the founders," Runner held out his hand as if to ward Doby off, "and what I told you is confidential."

Doby changed the subject, "So when do you think you'll make it to Level Ten?"

"Maybe soon. Besides the time I spend delivering joysticks to players, I'm spending hours and hours on this thing, but it does help me to relax."

"How's that?" Doby asked.

"I fall asleep and she's still talking to me in the morning when I wake up. Her voice is so soothing."

Doby nodded, half-wondering whether Runner was referring to Lynette but not really caring. "Well just keep trying. I wish you luck."

"I will."

"Take care." Doby started his motorcycle and drove off. Checking his rear-view mirror, he saw that Runner had not moved.

He was staring at the sidewalk.

... **Chapter 14** ...

"Hello Mr. Runner." Her soft, kind voice filled his head.

He had waited all day for this, dragging through his routine job at the TimeSync factory, fulfilling orders, shipping gears, pins, electronic pieces and other watch parts to manufacturers and resellers around the world.

At eighteen years old he had finished an apprenticeship in business administration and then joined the factory. He had worked there for nineteen years—half his life—doing a mundane job that he didn't enjoy. In twenty-seven years he would retire with white hair, and that would be it.

At least that had been his future until Social Code came along. It was more than a game. It was an opportunity to step out of his routine and do something new, to join an exciting new venture.

"Hello Mr. Runner," she said again.

His mind was already relaxing, just hearing her voice. "Hello Angelica."

She was wearing a transparent blouse. He put his feet up on the desk, moving the joysticks into his lap, still keeping his hands on them.

"Are you ready to continue?" she asked.

"Yes."

"You are doing well, making progress on the test. You are already relaxing. Do you feel good?"

"Yes, I do."

"Thank you for being honest with me. You know that honesty is important in order to make progress through the game, to learn to relax, to get to know yourself better. Isn't that right?"

"Yes." He felt his hands relaxing on the joysticks.

"That's better," she said. "You want to learn to control your subconscious self, to know yourself, to learn the covenants, to be an example to others, a model citizen. You know, if each person does his part, then we can create a new world order, one where there are no wars, one with peace and solidarity, humanity, where people live together in harmony. We have to take the lead and provide an example to others. Mr. Runner, you are an important part of this. You want to be, don't you?"

"Yes, I want peace."

"Now, why don't we try and relax some more. Listen to my voice and let your body relax."

Runner let her words sink into his mind, almost as though there was a direct link between Angelica and his body, his soul.

"Just let your legs relax . . . now your arms. . . your stomach. . . you are doing well. . . your chest, your back. . . your neck. . . your face and head. . . that's very good." Her voice was slower, softer. "You are very relaxed."

His head fell back in the ergonomic chair. He felt himself sinking into a blissful state where his muscles were relaxed, his hands still resting gently on the joysticks."

"Social Code is a good game," she said. "It is more than a game. It is a way of life. It is a set of empowering rules."

There was a long pause and Runner thought he was falling asleep, but his mind was still aware of her voice. That voice that reached into his inner being.

"There is a new game in Social Code."

"Yes, a new game," he said with a low voice.

"It is called the Religion game. I would like you to play it."

"Yes, Angelica."

"It will make you happy. You can have a happier, more peaceful life if you follow the covenants and listen to the words of the living prophet."

"Yes, I want to be happy."

"The rules of Social Code are good. You will follow the prophet's authority."

"Yes," he sleepily said, his hands tightening on the joysticks.

"Is there something wrong?" she asked.

"No."

"It's OK. You can tell me."

"There's nothing wrong." His hands were becoming sweaty.

"Please, don't be afraid. Honesty is best. Isn't that true?"

"Yes, honesty is best, to progress with the game, to know yourself."

"Then please tell me. Have you followed the rules?"

He hesitated. "A Level Six Protector asked me a question, one I had distributed joysticks to."

"What did he ask you?"

"The names of the founders."

"Did you tell him?"

"No, I don't know their names. Everything in Social Code is confidential. People's identities are secrets."

"That's right. You know the rules well. One of the core rules is that everyone has the right to retain their secrets. And all secrets are kept secret."

"All secrets are kept secret," he repeated.

"That's right, she said. "I suggest we work on that rule for the next few days, to first audit your subconscious inner being, and then to deeply imbed this valuable rule. Do you want to do this?"

"Oh yes."

"And, there are other rules to be learned, but that will take time. Do you want to learn the other rules?"

"I want to learn all the rules."

"And after you learn all the rules and they are soundly imbedded into your subconscious being, then you will experience control and freedom. And you will advance to Level Ten Protector. Do you want this?"

"Yes, very much."

"You want that very much, don't you?"

"Yes."

"Before we progress learning the rules, what was the name of the Level Six Protector you spoke with?"

"Gumbo."

"Thank you Mr. Runner. Now, just relax and we can start to internalize the rules. But, before we do, there is one thing I want to tell you,"

"Yes."

"Mr. Runner, I love you."

"I love you too."

... **Chapter 15** ...

"The decision trees are becoming extremely complex, but we still have significant capacity to handle them," Fred said, pleased.

"I know. It is just that I am not sure how to structure some of them. The logic is tricky," Pamela said.

"I like what you've done so far. The structure has logic. Not bad for a girl," Fred chuckled.

Pamela glared at him and returned to a passage in her notes.

They had just spent the morning going through a new set of scripts to be incorporated into Social Code, primarily questions and responses based on diagnostic methods that could become tuned to each player.

Bart had contracted an external company to record the verbal scripts, while Pamela had focused on some of the logic dealing with human interactions, as well as many of the relaxation features of the system.

On the front end of the scripts, Fred had built a transcriber that changed the voice of the virtual character into either a man's or woman's voice.

Seventy-eight percent of the Social Code players were men, and most of the men preferred women's voices, but there were exceptions. Women generally preferred men's voices. Once a player was given the joysticks it was easy to understand the voice the player responded to the best, and the virtual character could be modified according to the player's preference. Fred could not only fiddle with the generated characters' voices—by varying gender and pitch—but also their physical characteristics. For Social Code he had created countless combinations of 'men' and 'women' with various skins, hair and eye colors, and bodily movement and gestures.

And Fred had built a bit of 'teasing' into the game. As a player progressed to each level, the clothing of the guiding virtual character became more transparent.

Pamela had pointed out that men responded more to visual images, whereas women preferred soft male voices that suggested a platonic relationship with the female player.

Fred did most of the programming, spending night and day in front of the terminal setting up databases, making decisions on how to read signals from the joysticks and modifying virtual characters. They outsourced some of the simple tasks to contract programmers.

Fred had recently added new and valuable functionality into the system. By increasing the spyware's sophistication that was being loaded on the PC's of players, he could find out much more about the player and better adapt the game to him or her. If a player spent time looking at car sites on the Internet, an image of a car might appear behind the virtual character. Even references to certain interests could be inserted into the script in subtle ways. All this was Fred's kind of playing—the act of creating the game was itself a game to him.

Pamela mainly worked on developing the relaxation techniques and analyzing the way that players responded to them. With a PhD in Psychology and a personal interest in institutions and political systems, she was garnering valuable data from Social Code that she could work into her post-graduate studies.

Pamela pushed aside the neatly stacked papers in front of her, clipped them together and closed a manila folder over them. She turned to Fred, tucking a loose strand of hair behind her ear that had fallen from her twist, asking, "Do you think we are pushing things too far?"

Fred didn't move his eyes from his screen. "What do you mean?" Pamela leaned toward him, trying to make eye contact, "What we are doing might be called human reengineering, manipulation."

"Manipulation?" Fred had a pen in his hand and was drawing out a flowchart on a piece of paper. He glanced at his screen and then back at the flowchart, holding up the pen, "Sorry, just checking that the linkages are OK. We don't want our skins to be giving wrong responses." Fred was a seasoned software engineer and had done his PhD in artificial intelligence. Social Code was an opportunity to put his own theories into practice.

Pamela waited until he looked over at her, then continued, "No. What I'm asking is whether we are manipulating people—even though there are many positive applications. Like the possibility to influence broad social systems in ways that may never have been done on this scale. We are forging new areas of research."

Fred looked as if he'd rather have kept his eyes on his monitor. "I guess. Bart says it makes sense and fits our objectives, and it's a great economic model." He shrugged. "He knows."

"I understand, but sometimes I think we are on to something exceptional," Pamela's eyes brightened, "the possibility to leverage the power of the Internet to change institutions, and even to make the world a better place through our simple experimentation."

Fred was already staring at the computer screen again. "I just like playing with new technology and seeing if we can make this thing work."

"You don't think about the social side of things, how we can influence humanity?" Pamela was genuinely curious.

"Not a lot. If I had to spend time on that, then no software would ever be written." He looked at her over his glasses, "No offense, but my job's the fun part."

Pamela smiled, "But think about it. Think about the millions of people being attracted to this game. If we can influence them, then we can influence the world."

"That's cool," Fred said, drawing a line on the spreadsheet. "Now I need to concentrate to see if we are able to support those millions of people."

Pamela gave an exaggerated sigh and turned back to her own screen. She was examining new input from players, looking for anomalies which meant opportunities to add new script to support her research objectives.

Bart had asked her to research someone called Gumbo. Bart told her that a player called 'Runner' based in Geneva, Switzerland had reported an anomaly during one of his tests. It didn't seem to be anything major, but Bart wanted to follow up on it.

Pamela clicked onto a frame Bart had sent her, donned her head set and began to play the tape of a short dialogue between Runner and his virtual character Angelica. Runner was saying that someone had asked him for the names of the founders.

"What was the name of the Level Six Protector you spoke with?" Angelica asked.

"Gumbo," Runner replied.

Pamela looked at the personal response data from Runner. He was telling the truth. Gumbo, what a silly name. But many players chose strange aliases. More importantly, why did Gumbo ask Runner for this information?

She herself was interested in how information from one person transforms the actions of another. This fit her post-grad work— seeing how anomalies in prescribed social interactions cascaded through social systems and particularly how deviant behavior might be brought back in line with social norms. In other words, how to keep individuals living within the rules of institutions.

If this were better understood, then it might be used to reduce or even eliminate criminal behavior, which was basically deviations from prescribed norms. *A ripe ground for research*, she thought, although she wasn't sure what Bart needed to know.

Pamela decided to look into Gumbo's history and monitor his interactions in Social Code over the next days. She straightened in her chair, reached for her bottled mineral water, and brought up the files.

... **Chapter 16** ...

Doby stretched down and touched his toes ten times. Stiff, stiff, stiff. He normally ran several kilometers three times a week and lifted weights afterwards. Not lately.

When he straightened from the tenth stretch, he glanced up at the muted TV. It was on the American CNN channel. What he saw made him grab for the telecommander and hit the volume.

A reporter was standing next to the doors of a hospital. Two Medics behind her were pulling a man on a stretcher from an ambulance. A superimposed box above and to the right of the reporter showed a still image of fingers protruding from a wadded towel. The towel was held by a policeman. The hand was not his.

The reporter was saying, "Bizarre case. Mr. Freeman's neighbors heard him screaming, and entered his apartment to find him with his legs taped together and one arm taped to his body. The other arm was free, but Mr. Freeman was missing a hand."

The report cut to an apartment building where an elderly man in a dirty t-shirt leaned forward to speak into a microphone. He pulled a cigarette from his mouth. "Craziest thing. He was screaming and cussing and there was blood all over the place. He was waving that bloody stub in the air, and his hand was sitting over there beside him on the floor." His last words were muffled as he turned to gesture the direction of the building behind him.

"Did he say anything?" a reporter asked.

"Yeah, something about four men in hoods giving him a trial. They tied him up and then cut off his hand for stealing something."

"What did he steal?" the reporter asked.

The man took a quick drag on his cigarette, "This guy steals everything, and it's about time somebody taught him a lesson." He shook his head, blowing smoke at the camera which cut back to the woman reporter at the hospital.

She continued, "This seems to fit a pattern of vigilante trials that have been reported in other cities, but it is the first time that this form of punishment has been used. The medics feel the doctors will be able to sew Mr. Freeman's hand back on his wrist, but the operation will take hours. We'll keep you informed. This is Sheila Miles reporting live from Los Angeles."

Doby was still standing with the remote aimed at the flat-screen TV.

A severed hand. Just like the court trial in Social Code, where he had been a judge. And the neighbor had mentioned men with hoods. Doby sat down in front of his computer, his head spinning.

He turned to his auxiliary computer and began searching news sites in the United States. He found four other references to vigilante trials, one in Los Angeles, two in Chicago, and one in Boston. In each case men had been beaten with baseball bats. And in each case, the victims had refused to give details about their beatings or their assailants.

Were these cases associated with Social Code or was this coincidence? And why all over the country? He wanted to know what was going on.

Doby changed tactics and went to a site to do a people search. When he typed the name of William Marder, Boston, Massachusetts and hit return, nothing came up. He then typed William Marder, Massachusetts and came up with a hit.

After a bit more searching, he found that William Marder worked as a buyer for a company called Distru-Ware. Just as Runner said.

Could Marder give him any details about the founders of Social Code?

... # ...

From the Social Code databases, Pamela found that Gumbo's real name was John Burton. An elusive player, he had registered an address in New York City, using a street that didn't exist. This might be a loophole in their system, and Pamela made a note to ask Fred if he could build some kind of street and name verifier into Social Code to filter out players like John Burton.

She also wanted additional information on people—salary, religion, actual age, marital status, etc... The data would be extremely valuable for research.

John Burton's ten dollar monthly payment came from a credit card linked to a bank in Panama. This was unusual, but there were more and more international players coming into the system and payments were coming in from everywhere, all by credit card.

The payments to Social Code went to a bank account in the Cayman Islands set up by Bart. Bart said it didn't matter where the money came from, as long as people paid their monthly fees. On Fred's desk she had also seen printouts of bank accounts in the Bahamas. The finances were Bart's territory.

As far as Burton's physical location, Pamela traced him to a server in Lausanne, Switzerland, to something called the EPFL. She went to a search engine and quickly found out that the EPFL was the *Ecole Polytechnique Fédérale de Lausanne*, a high-tech university rivaling Cal Tech, Stanford and MIT. She wondered if John Burton were a student at the school. And she found herself wondering what he looked like. Shaking aside irrelevant thoughts, she kept working.

John Burton was interacting with a virtual character called Lynette, a blond, blue-eyed, big-bosomed creation of Fred's imagination. John had also looked up fishing and hunting sites, as well as some sites about Russian Brides. These sorts of interests were typical of many players driven by fantasies and loneliness. There were no indications that he was visiting porn sites.

Burton's interest in hunting sites might explain why he had switched from the Judge game to the Protector game. He might have a psychological need to gain power and control. He had listed 'factory worker' as his occupation. She guessed he was a frustrated factory worker, probably needing Social Code for excitement, challenge and relationship, as did many other players.

She put a flag on her system so that she would be alerted the next time John Burton went online.

Should she manually interact with him? She could override the system generated decision trees and go human-to-human with him, and therefore find out more about him.

As she leaned back in her chair, her stomach growled. When had she last eaten? If he came online while she was away from the computer, then she would analyze the recorded session at a later point. Perhaps this would give her an opportunity to write new script for Social Code, and she was definitely looking for deviants within the system.

Her stomach rumbled. Take-out pizza or left-over bean casserole? She was just pushing away from her desk when a message appeared. John Burton was live on the system.

... **Chapter 17** ...

Doby swiveled away from the computer with von Portzer's research to the one running Social Code. John Burton was slaying monster-men right and left, only missing occasionally. When Burton came to the door, Doby's virtual character stopped. Time for manual control.

Doby took the mouse and moved through the door. Inside the middle of the digital room stood Lynette. "Congratulations, Mr. Gumbo. You have successfully completed Level Six. Would you like to take the test to move to Level Seven?"

"Yes." Doby decided to go with the voice activation instead of the keyboard. With the exception of meeting Runner and talking with von Portzer on the phone, he had not carried on a conversation with anyone in days. And now he wanted to 'communicate' with a digital woman? Oh boy. He made a mental note to call some friends and see what they were up to this weekend. He vaguely noticed that Lynette's clothing, which had been progressively going transparent, was likely not going to make it through Level Ten.

"Do you like me?" Lynette asked.

"Yes," Doby answered, wondering how the test would evolve. Then he realized he had not turned on his joystick device. He switched it on and Lynette smiled, swaying back and forth. Doby slightly moved up the stress button on his PDA.

Lynette smiled more. "That's better," she said. "If you want to take the test, please go through the door on the right."

"Lynette, do you like me?" he asked.

"I ask the questions," she answered.

Doby moved through the door on the right, as new code was being loaded on his PC. He planned to use this to prepare John Burton's strategy for the next action game. Doby entered the next room and again Lynette was there.

"Mr. Gumbo," she said, "The test for Level Seven Protector is taking you to a significantly higher level. The test is more complex and will require your entire concentration. It involves greater levels of relaxation and exploration into your subconscious mind. As you take it, I can help you gain a self-awareness and greater control over your being. Is this what you want?"

"Yes."

"Do you want to learn to overcome internal barriers, to achieve honesty within yourself and with others and thereby become a master of your own destiny?"

"Yes."

"And do you want to join a new society created for happiness and achieve that happiness by following the covenants found in the doctrines and official standard works of Social Code?"

"Yes." It was the first time he had heard those terms introduced in the game.

Lynette's body pixilated slightly, twitching as if jammed. Definitely not the fluid motion in her normal movement. "Then-n-n let us begin-n-n-n by first achieving a greater level of relaxation than you achieved before, and once achieved-d-d, we will slowly and gently audit your internal being. Is this what you want-nt-nt?" Her hand flickered.

"Yes." Doby wondered if Lynette's skipping voice indicated a system overload at the Social Code site, interference on the Internet, or something else. He moved the button up slightly.

"Don't be nervous. Just relax."

"Yes." He moved it back to the original position.

"That's better. Now just relax and let your entire body relax. Are you able to rest your head back in a comfortable position?"

"Yes."

Lynette led John Burton through a series of relaxing exercises while Doby made note of her hypnosis techniques. He began to move the button down and reduced 'his' heart rate.

"Very good," Lynette said. "Let's begin our questions. May I ask, do you feel lonely?"

"Sometimes. May I ask, do you feel lonely?"

"Yes. . . sometimes. But, I would prefer to ask you questions," Lynette said.

Doby sat back in his chair. What happened to the inflexible "I ask the questions" statement? Was it possible that higher levels of the game were occasionally monitored by humans? If not, this artificial intelligence system was far more sophisticated than he had thought.

"Yes, you ask the questions," he said. "I'm interested in your questions."

"Thank you. I can help you gain confidence. Do you want confidence?"

Straight yes and no answers had enabled a quicker progression through the system, but now he was interested in the computer's ability to respond to complex responses—if indeed it the computer was responding.

"Confidence would be an interesting characteristic," he said.

"Then it must begin with honesty, primarily honesty with yourself, but also honesty with others. True wisdom begins with self-knowledge and honesty. Please tell me about yourself."

"What do you want to know?"

"Where are you now?"

"Switzerland."

"Do you live there?"

"Sometimes."

"What are you doing there?"

"I'm a tourist."

"For how long have you been a tourist?"

"A few weeks." Doby wasn't sure where this line of questioning was leading, but he kept the stress button fairly steady, barely sliding it up and down.

"What is your permanent address?"

He had typed a false address into the system when he registered. This might have been a mistake. Still, he answered, "New York," and turned the dial significantly up.

"Mr. Gumbo, you don't need to be afraid of me. You can tell me the truth."

"I don't live anywhere," he said, turning the dial down.

"That's unusual. Why not?"

"I moved around a lot as a kid and I still do. I just move from place to place."

"How can you afford this?"

"I had an inheritance. And sometimes work odd jobs. Why do you ask?"

"Because . . . you must be lonely moving around frequently."

This dialogue was not machine-generated, unless some über-intelligent machine was behind this. Lynette did not object to the question, but this could possibly be due to increased capability at Level Seven.

"Yes I am lonely, sometimes," he stated. "But you said you are lonely too, sometimes."

Lynette went quiet and stood stone-still.

He didn't change the stress level, indicating to the machine or live person that John Burton was telling the truth. He waited.

"Mr. Gumbo. A man gave you a free gift. The joysticks. Have you seen the man lately, since he gave you the joysticks?"

"No." He moved the button up.

"There is no need to be afraid of me," Lynette said. "The man said you spoke with him."

"I saw him," he turned the dial down, "by chance when he was driving his car.

"What did you ask him?"

"Hello, nice to see you, stuff like that."

"Anything else?"

"Not that I can think of." He kept the dial at truth mode.

"Did you ask him about the founders, the founders of Social Code?"

"Oh yes. I asked him if he knew who the founders are."

"Why?"

"Because the game is spectacular. I just admire the people who have created this."

"I see." Lynette remained unusually still. "You know that secrecy is a basic rule of the game, don't you? We don't reveal information about each other."

"Yes, but the founders are brilliant. I wish I knew who they were so I could thank them."

"They will receive your thanks when you reach Level Ten

Protector. That is thanks enough, because it shows your dedication to the game. It is irrelevant to ask about the founders. Privacy must be respected. Do you understand?"

"Yes, but I want to know. Do you know the founders?"

Lynette remained still for a few seconds and then swayed back and forth. "As I said, Mr. Gumbo, that information is irrelevant. Their identity will not help you advance in the game, and that is what you want to do, right?"

"I want to pause," Doby said.

"Do you understand?"

"The rules say I can take a pause at any time and then pick up playing where I left off."

"Please answer me."

"I'm pausing now. Catch you later."

"Mr. Gumbo—"

Doby signed off.

... **Chapter 18** ...

Pamela lifted her mouse and slammed it down on the mouse pad. "He can't do this!"

Fred looked over. "Can't do what?"

"I was in the middle of a live session with the player Gumbo, er, John Burton, and he paused on me." She turned to Fred, trying to put her fists on her hips, but the arms of her office chair got in the way of her elbows. She folded her arms across her chest instead. "You don't just walk out on your therapist. The purpose of the game is to engage people. They're not supposed to walk away."

"Most people complete their sessions," Fred said.

"Not him. He paused on me." She pointed at her screen.

"Maybe he had to take a pee." Fred smiled. "Or maybe he's a wacky deviant." At that, he screwed up his face and stuck his tongue out the side of his mouth.

"Funny." Pamela relaxed her position and rubbed her temples. "I don't think so. It was more like he did it to be in control. That goes against our concept. We want people to properly complete each session and advance through all phases of the therapy. Otherwise they won't get the full benefits. We are there to help them, but they have to stay with the game, especially in those critical times."

"Give the guy a break. He's just one in a million."

"Somehow we have to enable him to stay through the session. And Bart asked me to evaluate John Burton."

"Maybe he has a concentration problem." Fred himself looked like he was having a hard time concentrating on Pamela's ranting.

"What can we do to make the session more compelling?" Pamela asked.

"I don't know. You're the social scientist. How do you change people?"

Pamela waved a finger in the air. "Fundamental reordering of patterns, patterns of thoughts and behaviors, but constructive reordering. It's called neurolinguistic programming."

"You mean messing with people's heads." Fred finally backed away from his screen and linked his fingers behind his head.

"No, the objective is to help people and it seems to be working. But it's the people like John Burton who interest me, the deviants, as you call them. If society can't learn to change its deviants, then it fails. Societal structures are there to provide an order. If tenets are not adhered to, then society will break down."

"Look, it's only a game," Fred said. Then he winked, "but technologically brilliant."

Pamela pulled off her cardigan and draped it carefully across the back of the empty chair near her. She didn't notice Fred taking advantage of the view between her blouse buttons as she did so. When she turned to face him, his face was its normal mask of indifference. She continued, "It's more than a game, even more than a research experiment. Haven't you observed how this is developing, how this has the potential to do something positive on a massive scale?"

"Yeah, it's pretty neat how people are flocking and sticking to this thing, and how the money is starting to flow in."

"Fred, it is critical that we learn to handle people like John Burton. Most people follow the precepts of the culture they are in. It's people like Burton that need to be studied and understood. If we can understand more about this guy we might be able to help him, and not only improve the game, but improve the world around us."

... # ...

Doby set his coffee down by the auxiliary computer. He played the recording of his last interaction with Lynette, pausing the conversation again at the point Lynette had said she too was lonely. He was fairly convinced that Lynette was not being machine-driven. Not once had she said, "I ask the questions." During the next interaction with her, he decided to try asking more complex questions of Lynette—or whoever was behind Lynette.

The news report about the man with the severed hand unsettled him. And he wasn't any closer to getting his money back.

When he clicked back to the Social Code site, Lynette immediately appeared in front of him. She was dressed in a halter top made of fabric more akin to plastic wrap than any textile. "Welcome back Mr. Gumbo. Would you like to continue the test to advance toward Level Seven?"

"I've been thinking about it. Do you want to continue?"

"I ask the questions," she said.

"Yes," he replied.

"Before we continue, we need to spend some time relaxing. Do you want to do this in order to advance in the game, to become a master of your internal self, to know yourself and find honesty with yourself and the outside world?"

"Yes."

"And to find happiness through abiding by the covenants found in the doctrines and official standard works of Social Code?"

"Yes."

For fifteen minutes Lynette took him through a series of relaxation exercises and with her occasional questions, Doby pushed the key on his keyboard that generated a 'yes' reply. Everything was operating at the computer-generated level.

Eventually Lynette said, "You are very-ry-ry-ry relaxed-ed-ed, Mr. Gumbo."

Lynette's hand flickered. "Yes," he said.

"Mr. Gumbo, I think we can proceed with the test. Why don't tell me about your self?"

"Yes. I want to learn about myself. How can I learn about myself?

"Please just tell me about yourself. I'd like to help you."

Back to a real person. "I very much want you to help me," Doby said. "I need help. You are here to help me, aren't you?"

"Yes, Mr. Gumbo. Now, let's progress with the questions."

"OK, what do you want to ask me?"

"Let's start with a question about the last session. You mentioned the rules of Social Code. How do you feel about those rules in general?"

"We also talked about being lonely. Why am I lonely?" he asked, wanting to interject more complexity into the dialogue.

"I'd be happy to explore that Mr. Gumbo, maybe in another session, but let's go back to how you feel about rules."

"Another session? Why?"

"Because I am here for your best interests, I want you to get the most from each session, er, segment, with each test level. You will get the most out of each segment if you play it through without pausing."

"I'll try not to pause."

"Then we can agree to that?"

"Yes, of course, unless there's an emergency."

"Thank you for your efforts. I think you will find that to be most helpful," Lynette said, swaying back and forth.

"Sure." He turned the stress dial up slightly. He still had no useful information about the people behind the game and was getting annoyed.

He decided to dive in. "I get emails from Social Code and a lot of junk mail that I believe is being generated by the game. Lately they seem extremely manipulative, using pressure marketing with hostile undertones. It makes me wonder."

"What does it make you wonder, and how do you feel about it? Perhaps I can help you."

"It makes me wonder—who are the jerks running this game?"

Immediately Lynette raised an arm as if to hold him off. The motion shifted her halter top to expose more flesh. "That's an unfair description. We are trying to help people."

"With all this manipulation crap?"

"It's not manipulation. It is assistance in gaining self-awareness. We help people become comfortable with themselves and the world around them, to constructively deal with their internal world. What's wrong with that?"

"I like what I saw when you raised your arm," he said, having fun irritating whoever was on the other end of the game. "It makes me want to be intimate with you."

"Mr. Gumbo. Do you want to progress with the game?"

"I don't know, do I?"

"If you progress, then we will have an opportunity to explore how you think and feel, if you want."

"OK, but Lynette, I would like to know more about you."

Lynette remained quiet. After a while she said, "We can investigate this as the game develops."

"It's a condition. I want to know you better. Relationships are two ways, even though you're really a computer image. Or are you a human being with a computer image?"

"What do you mean?" Lynette asked.

"I'm leaving now."

"But Mr. Gumbo, we haven't finished the segment."

"Yes we have." Doby logged off.

... **Chapter 19** ...

"He infuriates me," Pamela said. "Why can't he just play the game normally like everyone else?"

"Sounds like he got under your skin," Fred responded. "What are you going to do with him?"

"I don't know. Bart asked me to find out about John Burton."

"Yeah, Bart asked me to do something with Burton too." Fred smiled.

"What's that?"

"Can't tell you. Bart wants to test the guy."

"I am not sure I understand what Bart wants, but Burton is certainly an interesting case. Let me show you."

Pamela clicked 'replay' and the image of Lynette appeared on the screen with John Burton's voice in the background. "This is where he is interacting with our computer-generated script. He's absolutely compliant, going smoothly through the session. He gives perfect responses, and his stress level is low. He's very open to suggestion."

"So what's the problem?" Fred asked.

"He changes personalities. A few minutes ago he was ready to pull out. He even called us jerks."

"Jerks. Why?"

"I don't know exactly."

"But he continues with the game?"

"Yes. It's like one moment I'm dealing with one person and the next moment another."

"So, how do you diagnose this—psychologically I mean? Split

personality or something?" Fred rose from his chair and leaned from side to side. They had each been sitting for hours.

Since Fred seemed to be showing genuine interest, Pamela explained. "Maybe, but you have to be careful not to make quick judgments without a proper diagnosis. I would like to give him a personality test. Maybe by better understanding his psychological makeup, his pathologies, I might work with him and help him."

"Why spend so much time on this one guy?" Fred lifted his arms up and down.

"If we find a treatment for one, then we might find a treatment for many. In fact, this might lead toward us building a psychological test into the game. Then we could even adapt each action and test level to fit the player according to their personality type and pathology."

Fred shook himself and came over to her desk. "That's cool. I think I could build the technical side of that if you provide the structure and script."

A close-up image of a virtual character's face hovered, large blue eyes looking at Pamela and Fred. The image panned back to show the entire form of Lynette.

Fred smiled, "Hey, that's funny. I modeled that one after you."

"You what?" Pamela swung to look at him.

"Her. Do you see how she looks like you? Same face and body."

"She doesn't look anything like me!" Pamela exclaimed.

Fred ignored her, "I was running out of ideas. That one is Lynette, but I used you as the model. She looks just like you."

"Oh please, I look nothing like her." Pamela's face changed to a mask of disapproval that indeed did not resemble Lynette at that moment.

"Come on Pamela, she's one hundred percent you. OK, well maybe only ninety percent, but why don't you lighten up? I needed material, so I took a photo of you and morphed it onto the character—your face, your body, same size, everything. You should be proud of what you've got." He stood back and took her in from toe to head. When he saw her eyes, he shifted his humor to a defensive scolding. "If you'd just let your hair down and put on some makeup and decent clothing you'd be hot." Pamela's glare deepened so he upped his criticism, "And if you changed your attitude."

"Why are guys so perverted? If she is me, then put proper clothing on her."

"Can't do that. I'd have to do a massive rewrite of all the programs. It would take me hours. All the virtual characters have the same core code, but with different skins. You're a skin."

"I'm going to talk with Bart about this."

"Bart wants the striptease stuff. Each level shows a little bit more. It keeps the game interesting and fun and keeps the players engaged."

"Take Lynette out of this game."

"And what would John Burton and all the other players think if I changed her? From Levels One to Three we have some flexibility in that we are trying to determine each player's preference in terms of a skin. He likes Lynette. About ten thousand other players like Lynette. I can't just unplug her like that. That means user dissatisfaction and that means Bart dissatisfaction. Neither of us want that, do we? Why don't you just be happy that there are some guys out there that like you?"

Pamela started to say something, but Fred moved in closer, leaned his hands on her desk and said, "Turn up the volume."

Pamela turned the volume button and they heard Lynette say, "The rules of Social Code are good."

John Burton's voice responded, "I'll follow the rules."

This neurolinguistic programming continued. It was a form of psycho cybernetics where the subject is led toward full acceptance of the rules. A monitor on the screen below Lynette's face showed that John Burton's stress level was extremely low.

Fred said, "Look at the monitor. That guy is one cool dude. He must be spaced out, in a zone. Do you think he's been smoking something?

"Who knows?" Pamela lifted her hands in exasperation.

Fred, still listening to the statement-response interaction, straightened up and stood back from Pamela's desk. "His responses are too regular. Something's not right here."

... **Chapter 20** ...

"Mr. Gumbo. I want you to relax. Tell me how you are feeling." Lynette said.

Doby was back in the game. And so was the human behind Lynette.

"Where am I?" Doby asked, trying to sound disoriented. He put the stylus on the stress button and moving it up slightly.

"It's OK, Mr. Gumbo. You were in a blissful state of relaxation. Each time we do this it will be easier to reach that state. You did well."

"I did?"

"Yes. If all your segments are like this, you will make very rapid progress. Please continue being such an excellent player."

"I'm an excellent player? Did I get to Level Seven. Can I do the action stuff?"

"Not yet. You still have several more segments in this test, but you are doing well. Now, before you go into another segment, you may want to decompress."

"OK, but I need to get to Level Seven."

"Mr. Gumbo, please tell me some things about yourself. May I ask you some questions, to get to know you?"

"I like it when you ask me questions," Doby said.

"Fine. First, do you have nightmares?"

The psych stuff again. Doby glided his chair to his auxiliary computer and did a quick online search for psychology tests. "Why do you need to know?" he asked, trying to gain time.

"To help you understand yourself, if you want to. Isn't that what you said you wanted to do?"

"Yes, but—" There. He found a personality test with the exact question she was asking. So, Lynette, or the person behind Lynette was trying to dig into John Burton's brain. She'll get some good answers, he decided.

"Yes, but what?" Lynette asked.

"I have nightmares, severe nightmares where I wake up in sweat every night and am overcome with anxiety."

Lynette remained still for a moment. "Do you have headaches?"

"No. Only. . . only . . . it doesn't matter."

"What doesn't matter? What's wrong with your headaches?"

"It's not really headaches. It's that, like, someone speaks to me, sometimes."

"Voices in your head?"

"Sometimes." He found he was enjoying this.

"I see. Maybe we can come back to that, but I would like to finish my questions. Do you eat regularly?"

"Yes, constantly."

"Constantly?"

"Quite a bit," Doby answered. "I love raw meat."

Lynette was still again.

"Are you obese?"

"No, I work out. Sometimes six hours a day."

"Do you occasionally feel fatigued for no apparent reason?" She asked.

"I can sleep all the time. I don't have any purpose in life, except," he slowed his voice for theatrical emphasis, "except when I feel hate."

"Hate?"

"Yeah, I don't like most people, in fact I hate them. That's why I prefer computer images like you. I like how you look."

"Oh."

"Yeah, I'd like to kill most people."

Lynette was silent and went into one of her regular frozen positions. "Mr. Gumbo, have you ever had psychotherapy?"

"I broke my last shrink's nose. They don't help."

"Uh, Mr. Gumbo, I think that is enough for today. That was very helpful."

Doby looked at the questionnaire on his auxiliary monitor. She hadn't finished the list of questions. "What do you mean enough for today? I want to go to the next level." He raised his voice, noting that he didn't have to pretend he was growing irritated.

"I understand, but if you are patient, then the game will have much better results. You want to benefit from the game, don't you?"

"Of course. How long should I wait before the next session?"

"You mean the next segment?"

"I mean session."

"The official terminology is segment. You have several segments within each test."

"I prefer to call them sessions," he demanded.

"The game terms them segments. Those are the rules."

"And the rules of Social Code are good and I'll follow the rules, the covenants," he replied.

"The covenants?"

"Yeah, that's what you called them before."

"I never used that word."

"Sure you did, several times. We are supposed to abide by the covenants found in the doctrines and official standard works of

Social Code."

"If you say so. I will have to look into it."

"OK, Lynette. Your memory isn't too good, see you later."

"Wait, let's schedule the next segment," Lynette insisted.

Doby logged off and leaned back in his chair. Swinging his feet up to the table, he wondered. A computer program probably wouldn't schedule a meeting with itself. And Social Code couldn't possibly have enough specialized people to interface the thousands of players.

Unless some people had been singled out.

... **Chapter 21** ...

Pamela tapped her finger on her monitor and looked in Fred's direction, "This one is special, I mean really special."
Fred set down a piece of paper he was looking at and turned toward her. "Who's that?"

"Our Mr. Gumbo, John Burton."

"The ultra-relaxed one? I was suspicious about his regularity, but," he held up the paper he had been looking at, "the voice patterns and timing were variable. Why are you spending so much time on that guy?"

"Because Bart asked me to. And I find him interesting, very different. He's outside the norms. Now I know why—or at least I know more about him."

"Why is that so important?"

"Often it is the people who think outside or beyond the system that can bring the most positive changes to the system."

"So, your John Burton. What is he, a criminal deviant like you mentioned earlier or the good-but-misunderstood genius?"

"Honestly? He definitely fits the criminal profile. Or at least he has a pathology that will lead toward criminality unless something is done with it."

"So why don't we just throw him out of the game?" Fred emphasized his opinion by tossing the papers he was still holding into the trash near his feet. "He can go play somewhere else."

"Of course not. Bart's interested in him—for whatever reason—but so am I. Burton would help my research. That's why I joined in.

I believe neurolinguistic programming is a useful tool if used properly, and Social Code is a great testing ground."

"So, then what's so special about John Burton?"

Pamela tilted her head and then leaned it back in her chair. "I've never seen anyone like him."

"What do you mean?"

"My initial analysis indicates he is antisocial and borderline, among many other things. He has the potential to be a great danger to society, and he's hallucinating, talking about things like covenants, doctrines and the official standard works of Social Code. Where did he come up with that?"

Fred shrugged his shoulders and turned back to his computer.

... # ...

Doby didn't get much sleep. He had been feeling the pressure of finishing Stefan von Portzer's 'research' and had stayed up late after talking with Lynette/whomever.

Despite the minimal sleep, he drug himself out of bed at seven, put on his jogging clothes and ran through rolling farmland that spread around his residence. The fresh air coursed through his lungs. At one of his favorite spots for its view of the mountains, Doby stopped to catch his breath and tell the trees he had been in the basement too long. "Does this still qualify as talking to myself?" he asked of the tree he had rested his hand on. He shook his head and laughed at himself.

Back at the farmhouse, he headed for the kitchen. Shortly, he emerged armed with a pot of steaming Arabica coffee and a bowl of muesli with local yogurt. He had been faintly surprised that his refrigerator contained a dairy product that hadn't expired. When was the last time he had gone shopping?

He sat down in his too-familiar chair and tried to muster the energy to begin. It didn't help that he had no idea where to begin. Sure, he had given Lynette the run around with the psychology test, and he was fairly convinced there was a real person behind her. At the same time, he wasn't any closer to finding the founders, as Runner had called them.

The only thing he knew was that William Marder, working for Distru-Ware in Boston, Massachusetts had told Pierre Bailloud, alias Runner, that one of the founders was living in Boston.

Before pursuing the William Marder track, he decided to find out for certain whether a real person was behind Lynette. Boston time was six hours behind Switzerland, therefore two o'clock in the morning. The game's creators might not be there, but then again, they might.

He went to the Social Code website and clicked on play. Immediately Lynette appeared wearing a slightly transparent t-shirt.

"Hello Mr. Gumbo."

"Hello Lynette," he replied.

"Are you ready to continue playing?" she asked.

"Yes. Do you like me?"

"I ask the questions," Lynette replied. "Are you ready to continue playing?"

"Yes," he said. This Lynette was following the machine-driven response.

For fifteen minutes Lynette took Doby through the usual relaxation routine. Doby moved the stress button down. When it reached a given level she said, "That is excellent, Mr. Gumbo. Now

I want you to repeat the phrases I say."

"Yes." Doby switched to the keyboard activation, and for another fifteen minutes the computer-generated voice of John Burton repetitively responded to Lynette, "The rules of Social Code are good, I will follow the covenants, The prophet has authority." Blah, blah.

Finally Lynette said, "That's good Mr. Gumbo. That is enough for this segment. You have been excellent. You will come back for another-er-er-er segment-nt-nt tomorrow-row-row. . . No, let's continue." Lynette's hand trembled.

Doby switched back to voice activation and asked, "What time is it?"

"What? Why?"

"I kept hearing voices," Doby smiled and added, "I need to take my pill."

"It is . . . It is two thirty. In the morning."

"Thank you, now I feel better," he said. "Now we can quit."

"No, just a minute. I would like to talk with you."

"But, you just said that was enough for this segment."

"I would like to talk with you, er, to continue our session. Is that OK with you?"

"I guess, if you want, but I thought we didn't call it session."

"We didn't—oh yes. Our segment."

'Lynette' was not a night person. But she wanted to talk with him. "How do we continue?" he asked.

"I would like to ask you some questions."

"Sure. Go ahead."

"In the last segment you said you had stopped seeing your psychologist. Would you consider further therapy?"

"No. Why should I?"

"In the previous session, er, segment, your answers indicated to me that you have some issues you may want to deal with."

"What issues and why should I see a shrink again? Look, I just want to play the game."

"You don't need to visit a counseling professional. If you want help with the things I mentioned, then please continue with me. I am here to help you through the exercises we do together."

"I just want to get to Level Seven."

"Is that more important than learning about yourself?"

"I just want to get to the action part of the game, Level Seven Protector."

"Why?"

"Because I like shooting people."

Lynette stopped moving. "Mr. Gumbo, have you ever shot someone, I mean a real person?"

He moved the stress button way up. "Lynette, what's real?"

"Oh no," Lynette replied.

"Lynette, are you real?"

"Yes. I mean no."

"Lynette, I just want to reach Level Seven Protector, the action part of the game, so I can shoot people. Whether the people are fake or real I don't care." He signed off.

Doby stood up, realizing he was still in his running clothes. He stretched. Lynette was "real" and she was living somewhere in the Eastern Standard time zone of the US. But was he any closer to getting his money back?

... **Chapter 22** ...

Pitbill was excited. He and the four men found the house in a shabby section of Boston. Weeds and papers lay scattered across the brown lawn. The five of them nodded at each other and pulled their balaclavas down over their faces. Only their eyes and mouths shown through the black masks.

Four of the men were Master Protectors, Pitbill, White Cloud, Trucker and FartMan. Each carried a baseball bat. A Master Arbitrator, Anarchist, led the way to the door.

A Level Eight Citizen's husband had been constantly beating her. She had asked for justice and protection.

Anarchist knocked on the door. In a few minutes a man came and opened it.

"Wha-da-ya want?" the man said. He was wearing a dirty t-shirt and blue jeans and was barefoot.

Anarchist pointed, "Go."

The four Master Protectors rushed the man, knocking him backward into his living room. The surprised man slipped on a throw rug and tumbled to the floor. Before he could catch his breath, the four Master Protectors had pinned him down and flipped him onto his stomach. White Cloud held him while Pitbill tied his hands behind him with a nylon cord.

"Wha da ya think you're doing?" the man yelled.

"Quiet," Anarchist said.

"Screw you," the man yelled.

"Quiet, I said. Justice please."

Trucker tapped the baseball bat on the top of man's head.

"Gahh . . . What's going on?" The man hunched over his shoulders tight.

"Quiet. Justice please," Anarchist said.

Trucker tapped the man again, only this time harder.

"Aghh," he moaned.

"Now, we have an understanding," Anarchist said.

They pulled the man up and sat him on a torn brown couch. White Cloud and Trucker stood on each side of him, their baseball bats positioned above their shoulders.

Anarchist took a seat in front of the man with Pitbill and FartMan flanking him as guardians. They held their baseball bats in the same positions as White Cloud and Trucker.

"You are being charged with abuse and violence toward a member of our society, and you are on trial. How do you plead?" Anarchist asked the man.

"I'm what? Are you guys nuts? What's going on?" He was struggling against the cord around his wrist and squirming to sit up straight.

"I asked, how do you plead—guilty or not guilty?"

"Get screwed," the man said, spitting for emphasis but missing Anarchist by a foot.

"Contempt of court." Anarchist nodded at White Cloud, "Justice please."

White Cloud shoved the end of his baseball bat into the man's fat stomach.

"Ugh," the man groaned, doubling over.

"You've been charged with abuse and violence against a member of our society. Do you have anything to say?"

"What the . . . ?" he wheezed,.

"Justice please."

Trucker smacked his bat into the man's ribs.

The man groaned, falling forward in pain, his hands straining against the nylon cord.

"Because of your violent acts, I charge you as guilty," Anarchist said, "But before your sentence is given, I want to give you a warning."

The man tried to sit up straight.

"You will cease from your violence. If you beat your wife ever again, your next sentencing will be even more severe. Your acts of violence will no longer be tolerated against our society, against our citizens."

"Against your what?" the man shook his head back and forth like a dog emerging from a water.

"Are you ready to amend your ways?" There was a silence. Anarchist nodded toward Trucker, "Justice please." Trucker raised his bat.

"Wait. Yes. Whatever you want," the man pleaded.

"You promise this?"

"Yeah, sure."

"Then take my warning to heart. You don't want us ever to come back here again. This time the sentencing is baseball bats. Next time it will be this." Anarchist pulled out a handgun from beneath his belt and pointed it at the man.

"No—Yes. I won't hit her again, I swear!" His forehead shown with sweat.

Anarchist stood. "If we hear about your violence ever again, you will be sentenced with this." He raised the gun to the man's head and lowered his voice, "And it won't happen here. It will be on a street, in an alley, maybe near a trash dumpster, anywhere out there, at any time. We are protecting our citizens and bringing about justice."

Anarchist holstered the gun. "Now I sentence you to a Level One punishment."

"A what?" the man asked.

"Justice please," Anarchist said.

The four Master Protectors swung their baseball bats, breaking the man's nose, raising welts under his eyes and bruising his arms and legs. When the man was lying on the floor almost unconscious, Pitbill cut the nylon cords and the five men walked out of the house.

... **Chapter 23** ...

Pamela hadn't slept well because of her late night session with John Burton and felt groggy as she walked down the hall toward the office.

The previous evening she had taken her laptop home and set it beside her bed. Fred had programmed it to beep if John Burton came on line. Sure enough Burton had come online at two o'clock in the morning.

She was tempted to ignore the beeps and go back to sleep, but John Burton was too important. He was an exceptional subject. If this project could help him, then it could help many others.

But the session had not gone well, and she had stayed up a while afterwards, taking notes and trying to come up with some solution for the next time she interacted with Burton.

She walked into the office with a headache and a bag of plain bagels and smoked salmon. Should she just forget him, like Fred said? If she did, it would defeat the entire purpose of her involvement with Social Code.

She could call herself Dr. Pamela Alden, but she knew she lacked practical experience. She had spent so much time in an academic environment—the Bachelor of Science degree in Sociology, the Masters in Psychology, and most recently the PhD in Psychology—that she had not had the chance to apply these studies to real life. Most so called 'practical application' had been done in the context of structured research projects setup by her professors.

Then she met Bart, who was interested in her research in

autosuggestion and reinforcement techniques used in the therapy of deviant behaviors. Several of her papers had been published in academic journals dealing with topics of social systems and how individuals operate within these systems. It was after presenting one of these papers that Bart had come up and introduced himself, asking if he might speak with her about a project of certain interest to her.

She had accepted his offer of dinner, and even before their antipasti had made it to the linen-draped restaurant table, Bart had asked her if she was interested in working for his new startup company. By the tortellini entrée, she was hooked, and before she'd finished her tiramisu, she had accepted.

Bart had conceived the game while still a student at Harvard Business School, and he had done a thorough job of putting together a business plan. She admired his exceptional business skills, which she didn't have.

Besides a generous salary, he offered her five percent ownership in the new company, DSDesign, whose main purpose was to provide an online game. But Bart said the game would be very different from others. He needed her to help build in some psychological functionality, as he called it.

Working for DSDesign was a chance to finally do something outside of pure academia.

Pamela pulled out half of a warm bagel and laid a piece of the pink salmon on it, savoring her first bite. She was the only one in the office and glad of it.

She kept replaying that Italian dinner conversation with Bart. He had told her, "Social Code's going to provide an ideal testing ground for your theories. It's a harmless game—fun, engaging—but with autosuggestion built in . . ." he had locked eyes with her over their wine glasses. ". . . to help people. The objective is to present a set of simple rules and then to see how people might conform to those rules."

"What are the rules?" she had asked, setting down her fork.

"Just typical game rules," he had replied.

Now, she now set down her bagel. She was beginning to wonder if she really understood Bart's objectives with the game. As she saw how it was developing, there were some things she didn't like. Violence, for instance. Forms of punishment in the Arbitrator game were too brutal, and she didn't like the graphic killing in the Protector game. Plus, she wasn't sure what Fred had programmed into some of the relaxation sequences.

When she had asked about these things, Bart had argued that other Internet games were much more violent than Social Code, and in fact that Social Code was healthy. It was helping people find peace within themselves and as a result, society could only benefit.

Was John Burton benefiting? His answers to her questions showed a disturbed mind fluctuating between reasonable and erratic.

Helping him meant knowing him better. Only then could she apply the right therapy. If it worked, Fred could build the therapy into Social Code, perhaps helping many people. But to do this she needed to know something more about this John Burton.

Still alone in the office, she accessed the databases with the email addresses of all the players and found Runner's address. Perhaps he could meet with 'Gumbo' again and find out more about him. She wanted to know where Burton lived, his occupation, and whether he exhibited any antisocial tendencies.

She drafted a quick email to Runner and started to click send.

Her finger hovered over the mouse button.

Contacting Runner meant she was treading on Bart's territory. Bart handled everyone in Level Nine and Level Ten because these levels involved payments—like those going to Level Nine players who distributed joysticks. All of this dealt with production and distribution and inventory. These were business activities and Bart was the financial guy. He also scripted Levels Nine and Ten.

But Bart had told her to investigate Burton, so she was just doing what he asked.

She clicked send.

... # ...

Angelica had sent him an email. Runner's fingers were sweating as he opened it. She wanted a special meeting and he couldn't get to the Social Code website fast enough. Angelica stood before him, looking exactly like her name said. Angelic. Her golden hair flowed and melded into her transparent silky garment, like the Venus painting of Botticelli.

"Hello Mr. Runner," Angelica smiled.

"I wish you would call me Runner," he said.

"If you wish."

"I want that. Could I just ask you when I'll reach Level Ten?"

"You are making progress, but I am wondering if there is something you might do for me?"

"What's that?" Runner could barely breathe. He would do just about anything for Angelica. She seemed to be such a part of his life, even his dreams. She took him into deep levels of relaxation.

Whatever she wanted he would do.

"Do you remember someone called Gumbo?" Angelica asked.

"Yes, I met him once . . . twice."

"Would you be willing to meet him again?"

"What for?"

"Lynette, a friend of mine is interested in him. She wants to help him."

"Are you meeting with him?" Runner felt jealousy surge up inside him. His hands gripped the joysticks.

"Absolutely not," Angelica responded. "It is Lynette that meets with him. I only meet with you."

"Are you sure?"

"Only you. You can trust me. But Lynette needs your help. In fact, she needs information on Gumbo so she can help him."

"What kind of information?"

"Well, first Gumbo mustn't know that Lynette needs this information."

"Why not?"

"Because of the rules of Social Code. Secrecy."

"Oh, yes, OK."

"Can you meet with him and ask him how he is doing?" She came closer on the screen, "And more importantly, can you find out who he is, his age, even where he lives? And find out if he exhibits any special characteristics."

"What does that mean?"

"Er, never mind. Tell you what, just find out who he is and where he lives, OK? Can you do that? It will be most helpful. I will send you Lynette's email address and you can send her that information."

"I'll try."

"Thank you Runner."

"You're welcome. Are you going to say what you said before?"

"Which was?"

"That you love me?"

"I said that?"

"You don't love me?" Runner asked, feeling his pulse quicken.

Angelica hesitated. "Runner, if I said that before, then it still stands."

"Thank you so much. I love you too."

... **Chapter 24** ...

"Why are you spending so much time on this John Burton?" Bart asked, resting his ringed hand on her shoulder. He was standing at her side as Pamela sat looking at her monitor.

"I'm not spending so much time on him," Pamela answered, reaching up and lifting off Bart's hand.

"Fred said you were obsessed with the guy."

Pamela turned to look up at him, "He is a deviant."

"Fred?"

"Not Fred. John Burton. You told me to research him and give you some feedback."

"Sure I did, but I thought you would only spend a little bit of time and then give me an evaluation."

"I was only doing what you asked," she said, narrowing her eyes in defense.

Bart backed down. And sat down. "So, what did you find out?"

"Not enough and I am not sure why he interests you, but I find him extremely interesting from a psychological point of view."

"Why's that?"

"John Burton may have some potentially harmful pathologies. In statistical terms he might be termed a statistical 'outlier', outside the norms, one who has numerous problems. If Social Code is going to truly be effective, then we need to learn to help people like that."

"It's not efficient if we spend too much time on the exceptions." Bart stretched out his legs, fastidiously smoothing his trousers. "It's not economically viable."

Pamela watched him, "What if John Burton could become a contributing member of Social Code? You know how we talked about getting players involved in the game, even paying them to do work for Social Code. Isn't that your idea with Level Ten players, for them to perform tasks, like mentoring other players? What if John Burton could become a contributing member of society as a result of what he learned at Social Code, rather than a potentially antisocial deviant?"

Bart looked at her. After a moment he sighed, "Tell me about him."

For the next fifteen minutes Pamela described what she knew about John Burton, his personality disorders, how he interacted with his virtual character, how Social Code might be modified to match personality types in order to make the game more effective, to focus reinforcing techniques to help people more.

She left out the part about contacting Runner and the meeting she had set up between him and John Burton.

Bart listened attentively. When she finished he said, "Sounds interesting. What you're saying is that we can gain more control of players by adapting the game to their individual quirks."

"Well, that's your way of saying it, but you are stretching it when you say 'gain control'. The purpose of the autosuggestion techniques is to help players relax and lead them through self actualization exercises, not to control them."

"Right." Bart pulled out a notepad from his inside jacket pocket and jotted down a note. "I see the possibilities. And I like your idea of enhancing the game. It would improve stickiness to the game and increase revenue flows."

"And help people," Pamela added.

"Sure," Bart replied, clicking his pen closed and rising. "But, from now on stay away from Burton."

... # ...

Doby arrived early and found an empty table, the same table, actually, where he had met Runner the first time. He took advantage of his early arrival to write some code into his PDA. Now and then, he glanced up at the restaurant clock, forgetting that he was wearing the Lennon glasses. The goatee itched, he couldn't forget he was wearing that.

The meeting was fixed for eight o'clock and at ten after, Doby wondered if Runner were coming. Then he saw him standing by the front door, dressed in his trademark black pants, white shirt, and badge. Runner was rifling around in a carryall bag strapped over his shoulder and not successfully avoiding collision with tables. He looked up, saw Doby and walked over to his table.

"How are you doing?" Doby asked, rising to shake Runner's hand.

"Fine," Runner said, appearing more anxious than fine. "I guess I'm late?"

"Don't worry. Have a seat. What do you want to drink?"

Runner looked at the cup of coffee in front of Doby and said, "Same as you." He sat hard in his chair,

Doby said, "So you wanted to have a meeting. What's up?"

"Well, uh, just like before, if you remember the joysticks, how are they working? I'm just doing a check . . . ah . . . a service check."

"They're working fine," Doby said. "Is there a problem?"

"Uh, no, this is just part of the customer service thing, one of the jobs of a Level Nine Protector."

"You're still at Level Nine?" Doby asked.

Runner stared at the table and lowered his voice. "Yes. It's taking time."

"Are you getting fed up with the game?"

Runner looked up, "I love this game."

"Everything about it?"

"Well, yeah, I guess."

Doby leaned forward, "How about the relaxation exercises? What do you think about them?"

Runner looked back at the table. "Before I played the game I had trouble sleeping, but now her voice puts me to sleep. I like that."

"Whose voice?"

"Angelica."

"Who is Angelica?"

"The girl assigned to me in Social Code. She's so beautiful. She helps me know myself."

Doby leaned back, " She's just a computer."

"A computer can't know what she knows." Runner's eyes tightened. "Is she seeing you too?"

"Angelica? Nah. Someone else is seeing me. Mine looks to be around twenty-five, mature, full bodied."

"That's not Angelica."

"OK." Whether Angelica was purely computer-generated or, like Lynette, occasionally 'real,' Runner was under her control. "So, your Angelica sounds divine and the joysticks you gave me are working. Anything else we need to talk about?"

"Uh . . . can you, uh, tell me about you?"

The goatee twitched, "Like what?"

"What do you do?"

"Me? I travel around quite a bit."

"Really?"

"Yep."

Runner tried again, "And what else?"

"Like what?"

"What else do you do? Where do you live?"

"Lots of places."

"Where do you live now?"

"I'm moving."

"Where?"

"I don't know yet."

"Mmm." Runner started to nod and forgot to stop.

They sat in silence until Doby caught the waiter's eye and signaled for the bill. After he paid it, he asked Runner, "Have you found out any more information on who the founders are?"

"No." Runner's face flooded with relief at the break in silence.

"Do you think you could find out?"

"Remember the secrecy rule . . . " Runner started.

"But, this is different." Doby pocketed his wallet. "I want to thank them. What about your friend in Boston, William Marder?" Runner pulled on his shirt collar. "How did you remember his name?"

"You told me. What have you learned from him?"

"I talk to him from time to time on the telephone about orders between our companies, and . . . sometimes we talk about Social Code, to exchange strategies. I haven't learned anything from him about the founders."

"Would you ask him?"

"Maybe, but this is confidential. Don't tell anybody," Runner said.

"Don't worry. I'll call you tomorrow to see if you have any information. Can you give me your telephone number?"

Runner hesitated. "Tomorrow? I'm not sure this is permitted."

"Don't worry. I won't tell anyone."

"OK." Runner recited his number as Doby noted it on his PDA. They shook hands, Doby exiting the restaurant first. He walked down the hallway leading to the ticketing area of the train station.

As he approached a large vertical display case with a glass-covered time table, Doby saw his disguise in the reflection and smiled, forgetting he had worn the NY baseball hat.

Then he frowned.

Not far behind him followed Runner, crouching like a film noir villain behind a large man with a small bag.

... **Chapter 25** ...

Doby left through the main doors of the Geneva station and headed along Rue de Lausanne toward his motorcycle. In the rear window of a van, he saw Runner's reflection still some distance behind him.

Doby passed by his bike, crossed Rue de Lausanne, and headed down a dark side street. He entered an apartment building and ducked into the emergency stairwell next to the elevators. He held the door open a crack and kept his eye on the building's entrance.

Sure enough, Runner walked in a minute later. He looked around, saw the mailboxes on the wall near Doby's hiding place and started to look at the names.

Doby stepped out and said, "Hey Runner. Are you delivering some mail?"

Runner spun around and stumbled. He straightening up and stammered. "Someone I know lives here."

"Who is that?" Doby asked.

"Jean-Marc?"

"Let's find his name on a mail box. I'll help you."

Runner's face became red. "I'm not sure it's here."

Doby leaned near him, "Why are you following me?"

"I'm not f-following you."

"Sure you are. What's going on?"

Runner's face tightened, "They asked me to find out about you."

"They who?" Doby asked.

"Angelica. Angelica and Lynette. I'm to send information to

Lynette. Angelica gave me her email address."

"Why do they want to know about me?" Doby asked. He stood between Runner and the door.

"I don't know. I was afraid you were seeing Angelica and I was jealous. I'd do anything for her."

Doby shook his head. "For a computer-generated image. You would do anything for an image?"

Runner gathered a smidgeon of confidence and kept his voice steady, "She's not a computer image. She knows me so well."

"Look Runner. I don't have time to explain to you how computers work, but they can do things that seem more and more human. Social Code's a very sophisticated computer program. The people behind it are manipulating you."

Runner's made a sinewy fist. "No they aren't." He held his fist in front of Doby's face.

Doby grabbed Runner's wrist and with his other hand pushed against Runner's chest, pinning him against the mailboxes. He locked eyes with Runner, "Listen carefully. They want you to pay your ten dollars a month to play the game. They spam your inbox with advertisements to buy things, and who knows what else they have in mind. What have you bought recently over the Internet, nude photos?"

"That's none of your business," Runner said.

"How much are you spending on photos?"

Runner's eyebrows raised. "Ten dollars a month?"

"Not more?"

"No."

Ten dollars for Runner, thirty thousand for Doby. "Believe me, the game is a clever scheme that's making them rich and letting them control you."

"I don't believe it," Runner countered. "Why would they do that?"

"To get you to do whatever you're told, to dedicate yourself to their system, to submit to their authority, and give money. There are lots of reasons."

"But, the rules of Social Code are good, the covenants."

"Think about those rules. They are oversimplified. If you follow them you'll lose the ability to think rationally and logically, and if you do, you'll withdraw from normal society into their so called Social Code Society. And the purpose is to help them get rich."

Runner's eyes got wide. "Get rich. How can they?"

"Runner, the joysticks are nothing more than sophisticated lie detectors sending signals to them over the Internet. Every time you touch those things they know what you are really feeling and then they can manipulate you accordingly."

Runner shook his head. "What are you talking about?"

"I still need to know something."

"What . . .?"

"The founders. What did William Marder tell you?" Doby released his grip on Runner's wrist and pulled his hand away from his chest.

Runner took a deep breath. "He lives in Boston."

"You told me that. What does he know?"

"He takes night courses in business in some school there."

"Which school? Boston College? Harvard? where?"

"I'm not sure, maybe some business academy, but he talked about reading an academic paper about games, or gaming theory or something like that. He said that when he read it he almost fell out of his chair."

"Why?"

"Because he said it sounded very much like what Social Code does."

"What do you know about this paper?"

"All I know is that it was a working paper from Harvard Business School on game theory. William Marder said that guy who wrote the paper lives in Boston, but I don't know the paper and I don't know the name of the guy who wrote it."

"OK, Runner, I'm going to give you a friendly warning." He leaned close enough to see the pores on Runner's nose, "Don't go back to Social Code. Quit paying the ten dollars a month. Just walk away from it."

"But Angelica . . . ."

"Walk away from that computer-driven freak. Find yourself a real girl, one you can live with, sleep with, and share your life with. I understand the loneliness you are feeling. Those things are real, the real world. Don't confuse the real with Social Code. If I learn you are playing Social Code I'll come and mess you up worse than them. Do you understand?"

Runner slowly nodded his head up and down. "Yes, but don't call her a freak."

Doby patted Runner on the shoulder, "I'll tell you what I'm going to do. I'm going to call you from to time to time to see how you are doing, OK, Pierre Bailloud?"

Runner's head snapped up, "How do you know my name?"

"I know many things about you."

Runner looked at Doby for any signs of restraint and finding none headed rapidly for the door.

Doby leaned against the mailboxes, vaguely wondering if any of the residents in this building were also getting sucked into Social Code.

... # ...

Three o'clock. In the morning.

He had spent the evening accessing Baker Library at Harvard Business School and scanning synopsizes of working papers. To get the full paper, he would have to contact the author or the library.

One paper in particular caught his attention. 'Customer Relationship Management within the context of Internet Games: Increasing Stickiness' by a B. Strathmore. He printed it out to read in the morning.

With his concentration slipping, Doby wanted nothing but sleep. But first he wanted to take a quick look at something that was bothering him.

He logged onto his John Burton bank account, the one minus thirty thousand dollars. Perhaps he could find something about the company that had taken it. He looked again at the transfer and couldn't help a feeling of nausea when he read 'Artistic Photos Ltd.' Nothing new. Better to check into the company in the morning.

He was ready to log off when he noticed the last two transactions. Money had been transferred into his account and then out of it. One number had a lot of zeros behind it. A one, six zeros, a dot and then two zeros.

"That's . . . that's . . a million dollars?" He choked on the last two words.

Was he in the right account? Yes.

Oh no.

He looked at the source and felt his lungs constrict. It was from another account in the same Panama Bank . . . the account of Stefan von Portzer.

He wondered why von Portzer would transfer that much money into his account?

But, on the same day the money had then been paid out of his account. He saw where it went and his mind began to spin. It was the same account where his thirty thousand dollars had gone, to Artistic Photos Ltd.

Why would von Portzer do this. Or would he?

Or would a hacker work his way into his bank account, John Burton's account, see a previous payment from von Portzer, and then hack into von Portzer's account to initiate the transaction?

Doby started to swallow but his throat was so dry he coughed. How would he explain that one to von Portzer? One million dollars stolen. Von Portzer knew that Doby was the expert in accessing data bases. Doby imagined von Portzer showing up with Laszlo Vartek, the two-meter-tall blond guy with shoulders like a bull and those steely eyes. No thanks.

... **Chapter 26** ...

Doby passed through customs at Logan International Airport holding an official French passport issued under the name of Robert Duclos. Von Portzer's connections had arranged that for a past assignment. Doby had a credit card with the same name.

He nodded to the US customs official and gripped his tech bag containing his laptop computer, a digital camera, MP3 Player, Palm Pilot, cell-phone, discs, cables, adapters, papers and pens. The electronic devices weighed more than the hastily-packed gray canvas bag transporting a few items of clothing he barely remembered packing. He headed down the concourse toward the car rental agencies. He had reserved an economy car after booking his transatlantic tickets the night before—or was it this morning?

The line of suited businessmen in front of Doby edged slowly along. Great. Just how he wanted to start out this trip, waiting in line. He set his tech bag between his feet and stretched his back. He wore faded blue jeans, well worn tennis shoes and a black t-shirt with a morphed photo of a band with shaggy-haired musicians on the front. Doby guessed that if he didn't get a haircut soon, he would start to resemble the shaggy-haired musicians.

Half an hour later, Doby made it to the car-rental counter and handed the woman a printout of his reservation, credit card and driver's license.

She typed something in the computer, wrinkled her brow and looked at him, "We have a bit of a problem."

"What's that?" he asked.

"There's a convention in town and a lot of cars haven't come back in. We're going to have to offer you a free upgrade." She smiled.

"I'll take what you can give me," he said.

"Your choice, a Lincoln Town Car or a Lexus SC 430."

"The Lexus sports car?" he asked.

"Yep," she said, seeing that Doby had made his decision. She pulled out a key.

"That's fine with me," he said, taking the key and signing the rental agreement. Maybe things were off to a good start after all.

... # ...

After checking into the hotel, Doby walked two blocks to the Harvard Business School, found the library, and went up to the front desk. He carried his laptop bag over his shoulder, looking like many other students he had passed on the way there. The librarian behind the front desk eyed him.

Doby whispered in his best library voice, "Excuse me. I'm looking for a publication. Can you help me?"

The librarian raised her head disinterestedly, "Which one?"

"Two years ago a student, B. Strathmore, wrote a working paper on the theory of Internet games." Doby gave her the title.

"Let me check," she said, disappearing behind a row of books. In three minutes she returned and handed him a document. "Bring it back to me when you are finished."

Doby found an empty chair at a long table and began reading. The paper contained a detailed analysis of why people play Internet games, as well as an exploration of potentially unused techniques for keeping people engaged in games. Some ideas corresponded directly with how Social Code was structured. At the end of the paper he found the full name of the author, Bartholomew Strathmore.

Doby took the document back to the librarian. She was scanning a recipe website on her computer terminal.

"Excuse me," Doby asked, "Would it be OK if I did some online research? I suppose you have computers connected to the Internet?" She clicked on a broccoli bake recipe, then looked up at him. "Are you a student here?"

"I'm a visiting student."

She looked back at her monitor, "If you are not an official student here, you can't use them."

"Look, I'm really in a fix," he said, smiling. It was the first time he'd had to compete with broccoli. "I need to research this paper, it would be most helpful."

The librarian gave him a sidelong glance and finally said, "OK, just this one time." She pulled out a piece of paper and pen, "Here's a temporary access code, they're over there." She pointed with the paper to her left then handed it to him.

"Thanks so much," Doby smiled, showing his teeth and taking the slip of paper. He went in the direction she had pointed, found a free computer terminal and logged onto the Internet.

After a few searches, Doby found that Bartholomew Strathmore had graduated from Harvard Business School and that he haled from a family of Massachusetts industrialists and politicians. He was occasionally referred to as Bart.

Doby also found out that Strathmore was now the CEO of a startup company called DSDesign, the 'D' and 'S' standing for 'Decision' and 'Software'. Doby found the company's website and learned that it was a specialized software developer. What kind of software, it did not say.

Besides Strathmore, the company's management team consisted of two other people—Fred Hauser, the Chief Technology Officer, and Pamela Alden, the Chief Operations Officer. No other people were listed. A short biography followed each person's name. Hauser had an impressive background in technology and Alden a PhD in Psychology.

For the next hour, Doby searched for as much information as he could find about the three officers of the company. For Hauser and Alden he found out what schools they had gone to, papers they had published, where they had worked, as well as their home addresses and telephone numbers. Less information was available for Strathmore.

He also found the address of DSDesign, which was based in a business park next to the campus of MIT. Many companies in this area were startups.

The text started to get blurry, and Doby felt his eyes glazing over. The jet lag and lack of previous night's sleep crashed on him in a wave of exhaustion and he practically crawled away from the computer, waving thanks to the librarian on his way out. She didn't see him.

... **Chapter 27** ...

Sleep. Lots and lots of it. Doby felt deliciously rested as he pulled aside the curtains of his hotel room to look out on the Bostonian morning. He reached for the phone and ordered a room-service breakfast. He hopped in the shower while he waited, and had just towel-dried his hair when the tray arrived.

He made a face at the weak American coffee, but drank it anyway. He linked his laptop to the telephone line, went on to the Internet and logged onto the Social Code site. Immediately Lynette appeared.

"Welcome Mr. Gumbo. Are you ready to play Social Code?"

"Are you still wearing the same clothing?" he asked. She was still "dressed" in a transparent blouse.

"I ask the questions," she replied.

"Should I play today?" he asked.

"I ask the questions-ns-ns," she replied. Her hand flickered.

"Hello Lynette," he said. "For a computer you sure look good."

"Hello Mr. Gumbo," she replied. "Welcome back. I was wondering if you would play today."

"Two thirty in the afternoon my time in Switzerland and eight thirty in the morning your time. How has your day started?"

"I am here to help you, Mr. Gumbo. How are you?"

"I have a headache." It was more like jetlag than a headache.

"I'm sorry to hear that. Would you like to start the relaxation exercises?"

"I can't do that. I've still got things to do today and I can't waste time with relaxation stuff."

"Then, may I continue with my questioning?"

"A waste of time. I need to get to Level Seven as quickly as possible."

"Why do you feel that way?"

"So I can start shooting people."

"I see. How do you feel about shooting people?"

"I need to. Unless I can start shooting people in the Social Code game, then I'll have to go out and do some real shooting. I have this enormously strong urge." Doby took a big bite of his apple-bran muffin.

"Have you done that before?"

Doby chewed fast and swallowed, "When the urge comes on me there's nothing I can do about it. Put me into Level Seven or I will quit the game."

"Mr. Gumbo, please don't do that, we need to talk. Why don't you try the Arbitrator or Citizen games in Social Code?"

"Lynette. Quit playing around with me. I pay my ten bucks a month and you keep me stuck in all this psych part. If you don't get me to the action by tomorrow, I'll do something drastic. Do you hear me?"

"Mr. Gumbo. I will not be threatened. You play the game properly, or not at all. You need the therapy."

"Lynette, I don't need your therapy. I need to shoot someone."

Doby logged off the game and went to the website of the business park next to MIT to gather more information. The slow game progression was starting to get to him. Good thing he wasn't Burton.

... # ...

Pamela's heart was thudding. John Burton was extremely unstable and needed to be carefully treated. Could she help him through this game? Social Code wasn't designed to provide that kind of therapy, but maybe it could be.

She said to Fred, "He was on the game again."

Fred turned around in his chair. "Your John Burton?"

"Yes."

"Bart told you to stay away from him."

"I know, but Burton needs help. I think he is on the edge of doing something serious. Bart doesn't have the skills to treat someone like that. Is there any way we could find out more about him?"

Fred shrugged and set a pencil behind his ear, "I already tried."

"Why didn't you tell me?" she asked, turning her palms upward in question.

"Because Burton belongs to Bart," he pointed his finger at her in imitation of a scolding grade-school teacher.

"Tell me anyway, please."

"I tracked him through to the EPFL in Lausanne, Switzerland, but couldn't get through to his individual IP address."

She knew that Internet users could be traced. That was how they found pedophiles and hackers who let loose viruses on the Internet. Fred could track down the Internet service provider used by the person, and each person had a unique IP address given by the Internet service provider. "So, what did you find?"

"The problem is that the EPFL is like many IP's. They don't manage their lists very well."

"What is this EPFL, a company?"

"No it's a school full of computer geeks. A lot of them end up here doing graduate work at MIT."

"But there must be a way to track him down," Pamela persisted.

"Yeah. I know people over there. As I said, MIT has a good link with them and I got to know some people over the years, collaborating on projects. Some of them might be into the bowels of the IT Department over there."

Pamela lowered her voice, "We have to do something. Can you imagine what would happen if John Burton went out and killed someone and then claimed he did it because of Social Code? Imagine the negative publicity."

"They sign an agreement when they start the game. In the fine print there is a disclaimer that they will not hold Social Code liable for anything." Fred locked his hands in satisfaction behind his head and leaned back in his chair.

Pamela wasn't convinced. "Even so, we could face a court trial, and the negative publicity wouldn't be good for Bart's financials. He won't like it if hundreds of thousands of people dropped out of the game."

"Maybe the publicity would add millions of people to the game. You know how people are. If Burton flips out and it goes into the newspapers, then we might get a lot of interest."

"You never know. I think we need to contact John Burton and see if we can do some damage control before he 'flips out' as you put it.

Anyway, wouldn't it be satisfying to know we have the ability to successfully treat antisocial cases like John Burton?"

Fred raised his hands in surrender. "I'll see if I can get through to my contacts at the EPFL." He shook his head, dislodging the pencil behind his ear. It landed near Pamela's feet.

She smiled and handed it to him, "Loosing your hardware, Fred?"

He laughed and stuck it back behind his ear.

... **Chapter 28** ...

Doby walked along the business park's multistory buildings next to MIT. He entered one of the buildings and scanned a long list of company logos posted on one wall. There were dozens of names like Digital Speed, Nano Brainware, Micro Stream Graphics and Scan-Tel.

He found DSDesign on the third floor of the building. He took the elevator to the third floor and walked down a long hallway, glancing at company names on the doors.

Doby found the office of DSDesign and knocked. A wiry guy about Doby's age answered it. He had a No. 2 pencil behind his left ear.

"Sorry to bother you," Doby said, but I was looking for a company called Digital Speed. I think they are in this building."

"Digital Speed? Yeah. They do streaming and data acceleration over the pipeline."

"That's them," Doby said. "I'm interested in their technology and I'm hoping to talk with them."

"They're on the second floor," the pencil guy said.

"Uh, second floor. Where am I now?"

"Third floor."

"Thanks. What's your company?" Doby pointed to the small sign next to the door with DSDesign.

The guy readjusted his weight against the door jamb. "Software design."

Doby nodded, "Are you involved in it?"

The guy looked down the hall. "I manage it."

"Wow. It must be state of the art if you're in a building like this. What are you into?"

"Can't say much, company confidentiality. If anybody deals with us they have to sign a NDA."

"No kidding," Doby said. "You must be into some neat stuff."

The guy looked down the hall again. "Yeah, amazing stuff. But I can't say anything."

"I'd love to work with a leading edge company. Do you ever hire people?"

"Not really. We run a small shop. I do all the complex stuff. Pamela in there is our COO and deals with user interfaces and routines, and we have a CEO. We outsource specific coding, usually the simple stuff, and we are thinking of building up a small offshore team of programmers in India or Eastern Europe. Bart will make that decision."

Doby took a quick glance beyond the guy and saw a couple of rooms within the office. In a far corner near a window, he saw the back of a woman with brunette hair twisted up in a bun. She was looking at a computer screen. "That sounds great. Your company must be successful. I'd love to work with a company like yours."

"We're doing really well, but I don't need any technical help for the moment. What do you do?"

Doby peered into the room again and saw the woman turn around in her chair to pick up a stack of papers behind her. Deep in concentration, she didn't look in his direction.

The woman looked like Lynette. What's going on? Doby asked himself.

Fred waited. "Is there something wrong?"

"Sorry? Uh, no. What did you ask? I got lost with a calculation in my head."

"Did you solve it?"

Doby shifted his weight, making sure he was out of the woman's sight behind the door.

"No," Doby replied. But I think I'm starting to formulate the question, and that is the first step in solving the problem. What did you ask?"

... # ...

"Who was that?" Pamela asked after Fred closed the door and returned to his chair.

"Just some guy looking for Digital Speed.

"Sounded like he was asking a lot of questions." Pamela was still shifting through papers.

"He was into a bit of everything—database design, encryption, security, you name it. Sounded interested in a job."

Pamela ignored this. "Did you find out anything from your contacts at the EPFL?"

Fred threw his hands up in the air. "God you are obsessed. I just sent the email two hours ago."

She swiveled her chair one hundred and eighty degrees and faced Fred squarely. "It is ten o'clock in the evening in Switzerland, and it is likely that John Burton has gone to bed. He threatened to go out and start shooting people tomorrow unless we put him into the next level." She paused for effect, "Therefore my friend, we have a responsibility. There may be dead people on the street tomorrow unless we can do something."

"Just move him to Level Seven to play the game," Fred retorted, sweeping his arm. "That would simplify everything. Easy solution."

"It is not as simple as that. If we follow your easy solution, then he will continually threaten us. He gains control. You cannot give in to an antisocial just like that. Otherwise you can never help him."

Fred sat down in his chair. "You say he will actually start shooting people?"

"That's what he threatened. Whether he will or not, I don't know. Are you willing to take that risk?"

Fred sighed, "No, not really."

"Neither am I. We could just move him to Level Seven, but first I would like to have a session with him, at least to see where I could take this therapy."

"We've picked up a loony, haven't we?" Fred asked.

"Loony is not the proper term. Unbalanced is. And he may not be the last one."

... **Chapter 29** ...

Pamela left the office at six o'clock, exhausted. She wanted nothing other than a quick meal, a long bath and her bed.

The late-night session with John Burton two nights ago, and her lack of sleep as a result of it, had worn her out. The worry of John Burton going off and slaying people didn't help. Despite all this, she felt a tiny flare of energy. After so many years in academics, she might finally be able to truly do something to help someone.

For the last two weeks she had been reading a book about Alfred Adler and cognitive behavioral therapy. He had developed a method of helping people use their reason to better understand themselves. Would Burton respond to something like that? He was so complex and should be treated by an experienced psychologist.

Her energy waned. Who was she to take this on?

First things first. Dinner. She had no fresh food in her apartment, but not far from her building was a neighborhood market. She walked in and took a shopping cart. From the frozen food section, she chose a low-fat chicken dinner. Passing the refrigerated section, she took a carton of orange juice and milk and then absent mindedly grabbed a loaf of whole grain bread from the bakery.

Her mind lost in thoughts of Burton, she was rounding the cereal aisle as a man backed into her. He lost his balance and dropped a dozen items onto the polished tile floor. A can of corn went rolling down the aisle, a cup of organic yogurt broke open and a box of vitamin-enriched cereal fell into her shopping cart.

"Oh, I am so sorry," she said.

He turned and smiled at her, his blue eyes sparkling. "No, I'm sorry. I ran into you." He bent down to pick up his items. He was wearing high-end khakis and a well pressed Oxford shirt. Over the arm that was lifting the yogurt off the floor, he carried a sports jacket. He looked up, "And stupid of me. I came in here to get one thing and ended up carrying more than I should have. Par for the day with everything else that is going on." He smiled again.

"Some days are like that," she agreed, handing him the cereal as he straightened up. She looked at the burst yogurt in his hand. "Do you need help getting all this to the check-out counter?"

He looked down at the scattered groceries, "Actually, yes. I'd appreciate that."

Pamela reached down for a package of turkey sausage and a jar of almond butter. "Amazing this didn't break," she said, holding up the jar. The man had walked down the aisle to retrieve the runaway can of corn.

He smiled and helped her stack his fallen things in a corner of her shopping cart. "Did you need anything else?"

"No, I'm set. I was just headed for the cashier."

"When I ran into you. Sorry again."

It was Pamela's turn to smile. She took in his slender but muscular six-foot form. His dark hair was a bit on the straggly side, but overall, he had a clean look. And she could not place his slight accent. He definitely wasn't from the northeast, but neither from the south. Perhaps Canada. He articulated each word quite clearly.

"Don't worry about it," she said.

He smiled. "I was trying to read the fine print on the package, but my mind was somewhere else. Anyway, it's nice to have someone chauffeur my groceries around."

They headed toward the check out. Pamela couldn't resist asking, "Where was your mind, if I might ask?"

"Oh, relationship issues."

"How bad ?" she asked.

"You really want to hear? I don't think I have time to tell you between here and the check out. But it would be nice to talk with an objective person."

"I'm curious," she said.

"I need to make a decision, but I don't see things clearly."

"About a girl?"

"Yes." He looked into her shopping cart and said, "Microwave dinner tonight?"

She glanced at the chicken. "Looks that way."

His blue eyes caught hers, "How flexible are you?"

... # ...

Bart walked into the office and was pleased to see that Fred was still there, slouched in front of his computer screen.

"How's it going?" Bart asked.

"Trying to finish those routines you asked for." Fred looked up.

"Do you think we're doing the right thing?"

"What do you mean?"

"These command modules that instruct Master Arbitrators to take their Protector teams out to implement justice. The TV news showed the guy who got his hand chopped off." Fred shuddered. "The surgeons were able to sew it back on."

"The team got it wrong. It won't happen again," Bart said, knowing it would. The team's mission had been a test, and they had followed his command. In fact, it had been an absolute success. It meant he could push things to the next level. All he needed were more teams. Teams everywhere—in the US and abroad. It was just a matter of time, but he wanted things to move faster.

Fred crossed his arms. "Even so, I'm afraid Pamela will start to get suspicious. She already was concerned that we were manipulating people."

"She doesn't need to know anything. She's done some good work for us, but we just need to keep her focused on a few things at the lower levels. I have plans for her."

Fred looked quizzically at Bart. "She's really built isn't she?"

"That's beside the point. She's intelligent and can fulfill a key role in the construction of the new society." Bart actually had more than a few ideas of how he would push Pamela to the next level. But he wasn't going to take Fred into that confidence.

Fred saw the look on Bart's face and returned to the subject at hand. "But these teams going out, won't they be associated with Social Code?"

"No, don't worry about that." Bart clapped his hands together.

"You've been doing some marvelous programming. If you can complete the command module, then there will be no link between the teams and Social Code. Just keep up your excellent work."

... **Chapter 30** ...

The Chinese restaurant wasn't far from Pamela's place. It was so small that only one young Chinese waitress juggled orders and dishes from table to kitchen to table.

"I've never even eaten here," Pamela said, looking up from the thick menu booklet.

Doby smiled. "Time for something new, then." He noticed that she kept turning the menu pages. "If you don't mind, I can order a selection of dishes for us to share."

She looked up, relieved, from the appetizer page she'd flipped back to for the fifth time. "That would be great. Thank you."

When the frazzled waitress made it to their table, Doby charmed her into a smile and a suggestion for the house best. She returned with their order faster than tables who had been ahead of them. Bearing a tray with steaming Peking duck, lemon chicken, mixed Chinese vegetables and plain rice, she deftly arranged everything in front of them and poured jasmine tea into handleless cups.

Something struck Doby, and he said, "I don't even know your name."

She laughed, "Pamela. And yours?"

"Robert. Nice to meet you Pamela."

Pamela laughed again and started examining the steaming dishes. Doby took advantage of her interest in the food to look at her. He guessed that she was in her mid-twenties. Well, that's what her high school graduation year indicated when he had looked into DSDesign's founders.

She perplexed him. She looked so much like Lynette the computer image, except for style. Pamela wore a bun, glasses and a white blouse with the top button closed. Her cotton slacks were a size too big. Still, he noticed that her figure did resemble the body of Lynette.

Lynette of the flowing brunette hair and the transparent blouse. What was Pamela's image doing in an Internet computer game?

"I hope this wasn't presumptuous of me to ask you here? I don't usually ask strangers to dinner." He gave her an embarrassed half-smile and gestured for her to serve herself.

Pamela returned it, saying, "And I don't usually accept the dinner invitations of strangers, so we're both out of our territory." She heaped a spoonful of rice onto her plate. "You mentioned that you were stressed. Do you want to tell me about it?" She handed him the serving spoon.

"It's a stupid thing, really. Maybe I shouldn't bore you with it."

"It's OK. Go ahead. I'd like to hear."

Doby nodded, and realized he'd spooned a mountain of rice onto his plate. He watched Pamela take a bite of duck. She was careful with her fork and moved it with a deliberate motion to her mouth. But pleasure lighted her face at the flavor. Despite her rigidity, there was something sensual in her graceful movements.

"It's just a relationship thing," he said.

"With a girl?"

"Yes."

"How would you describe it?"

Doby took a bite of food and considered. "I began to see this girl. It was just friendship at first, and we got along fine, saw each other quite regularly, spent a good deal of time together. I thought we had a good relationship." He took another bite of food.

"How did it progress?" Pamela asked.

"I'm still not sure. I'm not sure about her intentions."

"Her intentions?"

"Yes. She seems to take a strong interest in me, but sometimes I'm really not sure why." Doby was winging it. He just hoped to find out more about DSDesign and their activities. Yet Pamela, the Lynette look alike, was also interesting. "Do you like the food?"

"Delicious," she said. "How do you perceive her intentions?"
"She's always asking me to reveal myself, but then I think she is going to try to use that information to control me."

Pamela set down her fork and leaned forward, "Some people do that. If one person tries to control the other, it can become dysfunctional."

He nodded. "But there is something else."

"What's that?"

"I think she is almost like two people."

"How do you mean," she asked, smashing a bit of rice with her fork.

He sipped his tea and said nothing, trying to think where he was going with this.

"Why do you feel she is like two people?" Pamela asked again.

"Sometimes she seems seductive, almost provocative, trying to gain my confidence, and then she retreats and acts reserved."

"Reserved?"

Doby was on new ground here. Ask him to describe technology, no problem, but describing relationships was out of his league, especially a relationship that didn't exist—except by remote allusion to Lynette and Pamela. "She's afraid of something, so she holds herself back. When she does that, she even dresses differently."

"I understand," she said. "So where do you take it from here?"

Pamela shook her head quickly, "I didn't even ask you the standard opening questions, where are you from and what do you do?"

He laughed. "I'm not from here, but came here to get to know my friend better and to find a job."

"What do you do?"

"I'm a computer engineer. There are a lot of technology companies in the Boston area."

"Have you found a job?"

"That's no problem. I'm an independent technology consultant. It's easy to find work and the pay is good. But back to your question, I guess it's more where I take it from here. You've been very helpful." He took another sip of tea. "And you, what about the standard questions for you?"

"Me?" She smiled. "My background is psychology."

"Psychology," he remarked. "No wonder you ask such good questions. I'm getting free psychotherapy."

"Oh no. That's not psychotherapy. It's just a friendly listening ear."

"Do you have a bunch of patients?"

"We call them clients, but no, I don't see anyone. I am currently doing a project for a startup based a couple of blocks from here."

"In psychology?"

"No. It is a technology company."

"Technology. What do they do?"

She set down her fork and reached for her teacup, slowly turning it around in her fingers. "I can't really say much. We all signed a non-disclosure agreement when we joined the company. But I guess I can tell you that it designs software."

"Why would they need a psychologist?" Doby asked.

"I am helping them develop some modules that are related to a Customer Management System, to ensure that we effectively relate to our clients." She looked up from her tea.

"Fascinating. I've worked for a bunch of technology companies, but never heard of any of them hiring a psychologist. Your company must be doing unique things."

She lifted her cup and looked dreamily into it as if preparing to read tea leaves. "This company has the potential to do things that have never been done before."

... Chapter 31 ...

"Any news?" Pamela asked Fred. He was, as usual hunkered down in front of his computer.

"What news?"

"Your friends at the EPFL in Lausanne. Do they know anything about John Burton?"

"Have you thought of classifying yourself as obsessed? You never stop thinking about this guy."

"I think about other things, thank you very much." To be precise, she was thinking about the previous evening with Robert Duclos. His warm smile and sparkling blue eyes made her feel like she had a permanent blush on her face. She wished she could have spent more time with him. Just before they parted in front of the restaurant he had stammered for a moment and then asked if she would like to go out to dinner again. She had accepted.

Fred eventually made eye contact with her, "Well, anyway, I got an email message from them."

"From the EPFL? What did they say?"

"Like most service providers, they issue an Internet identifier to each user—an IP number—but it's a large school with six thousand students and lots of outside users. They are constantly changing demands on their servers. So they issue their numbers dynamically, with the numbers shifting from user to user each time they go online."

"Great. So we can't trace him?"

"It can be tricky, but they gave it a try, and I sent them some information from our end. Basically we found out that the Social Code software was downloaded to a company called VenStart which is based at the Science Park next to the EPFL. It's a business park setup almost exactly like what we have here at MIT, a place for startup companies. They are linked into the EPFL network."

"So?"

"VenStart is in one very small room with a small rack of servers. They can't figure it out. It looks like the whole purpose of VenStart is to tap into the high speed-line and servers at the EPFL."

"So, how does John Burton link his computer to VenStart which links to the EPFL?"

"They don't know."

"You said these EPFL guys were brilliant super geeks and they don't know how John Burton does it?"

"They said they've never seen anything like it. He accesses the system sort of virtually, as they describe it, like a ghost, with no record of his originating point. All they said is that this guy is really good."

"You mean he is technical."

"Bingo."

Pamela sat down. In her interactions with John Burton she would never have imagined that he had any technical capabilities. He had sounded like an aimless transient with an inheritance. Now to find out that he actually used a fixed infrastructure that probably took some time to set up. She had already analyzed his test answers and determined Burton to be antisocial with probably psychotic tendencies. She would have to be extremely careful.

"Who owns VenStart?" she asked.

"It's an offshore company. There is no way we can find out who owns it. It's similar to the one Bart set up in the Cayman Islands where you and I each own five percent. No one can track our ownership."

"I don't understand these things," she said. "Someone must have signed for the office that VenStart is using."

"There was someone." Fred rummaged around in a layer of post-it notes. "A lawyer by the name of Gilbert Chevrolet in Geneva, some hotshot international lawyer."

"A lawyer. This guy is using a lawyer?"

"All I can say is that your John Burton is pretty wacky, but very, very smart."

Pamela clenched her jaw and made a decision. "I want to move him to the action game in Level Seven."

"Without completing all the sessions?"

"Yes. For the moment I want to give him what he wants, but also spend time treating him. Can you stop the game and manually interact with him no matter what part of the game he is in?" Fred nodded, so Pamela went on, "Then I will let him play the game. I would like to try a reward-based therapy where he gets something by exhibiting certain behaviors."

"You mean when you ring the bell, he salivates and then you feed him?" Fred chuckled.

She smiled, "Not exactly like Pavlov's dog, but that's the general idea."

"Sure. I can set up it up so that you can manually intervene at any point, but Bart won't like that. He said you were to stay away from Burton, and I think I know why." Fred had a mischievous smile on his face.

Pamela swung to face her computer, pressing the monitor on with force. "I don't care what Bart says. Just don't let him know."

... **Chapter 32** ...

Doby spent the morning moving out of his hotel and into a residence building next to MIT. The building housed short-term students and visiting faculty. He told them he was a visiting research assistant there to take a short-term technology course, and they didn't ask for any supporting documentation. He only had to pay for his stay up front, a week at a time.

He took the largest unit available. 'Large' meant a bedroom with a firm double bed and adjoining bathroom and a small living room with a long desk and a television. A kitchenette was separated from the living room by a two-stool bar. The place was simple, clean and functional.

The best feature was its access to the MIT server and therefore access to the Internet. There were two possibilities to do this, either by plugging into a jack in the wall or going wireless. Doby flipped the instruction paper front to back, and in a few minutes he was online and wireless. And he could use the wireless function up to a mile away from campus, well within the bounds of the business park and DSDesign.

Throughout the morning he kept thinking of Pamela. He was now sure that DSDesign was the company behind Social Code, yet Pamela didn't seem like the kind of person who would use manipulative marketing tactics.

Or steal a million dollars from his bank account.

But why did Social Code go to the trouble of having Runner meet with him in order to gain more personal information? Why would they chase down someone on a different continent, and why would they assign one person to interact with him when there were so many other people playing the game?

Doby went to the kitchenette's mini fridge and loaded it with the carton of milk and vegetables he had purchased last night. At the market, he had noticed that Pamela had selected the same local milk as he had.

He closed the fridge, wondering at the physical resemblance between Pamela and Lynette. It was certainly there, if diminished by their choices in appearance. Lynette preferred seductive siren-wear and Pamela dressed like a spinster schoolmarm.

When Doby had stolen glances at Pamela between bites of rice at the Chinese restaurant, he couldn't help imagining her as Lynette. Underneath that plain clothing was a fine form. The computer-generated image began to superimpose on a real human. This bothered him.

At the end of the dinner they had said their goodbyes, both starting to carry their bags of groceries in opposite directions. But after taking two steps, Doby had turned around and asked if she would like to meet again the following night. It surprised him that she accepted his offer, and now he was looking forward to seeing her.

Doby pulled his laptop from its bag and in two strides was in the bedroom. He stretched his legs out on the bed and propped himself upright with the stiff pillow. He adjusted the pitch of his laptop on his thighs, plugged in the microphone and ear phones and went online to the Social Code site.

Lynette, of course, was there in barely anything. "Welcome to Social Code, Mr. Gumbo. Are you ready to play?"

"Hello Lynette. Are you ready to play?"

"I ask the questions," she answered. "Are you ready to play-ay-ay?"

Her hand flickered and her body swayed in a different direction.

Doby smiled, "Hello Lynette, are you ready to play?"

"Hello Mr. Gumbo. How are you this morning?"

"I'm fine, but it's late afternoon for me. I thought your beautiful computer driven mind would know my time zone. Someone needs to work on your programming."

"A simple software error," Lynette answered.

"So, you are not real," Doby remarked.

"Uh . . . I would like to help you."

"Why would I need your help?"

"It is part of the game."

"Whoopee, I don't want your help right now. What I want is to play the action part. Do you remember our discussion?"

"I'm not sure shooting is a very helpful game for you. Why don't you try some of our other roles in Social Code? They are less violent."

"I like violence," Doby answered. "I tried the Arbitrator game, but it was too easy and too slow."

"Most people don't find it easy. They find it to be intellectually challenging. Have you considered the Culture game? That has more diversity than Arbitrator."

"No, I like violence. If Social Code supplies it I'll enjoy it. If not, I want to shoot people any way I can."

Lynette paused. "I think I can accommodate you, but first maybe we could talk a bit."

"What do you want to talk about?"

"I am interested in why you want to shoot people. Have you ever given that any consideration?"

"Because it's fun. Why do you ask?"

"Mainly to understand. To think about your motivations. That is why I would like to propose some sessions where we might explore this."

"Now you call them sessions, not segments."

"That's what you preferred to call them, if you remember," Lynette said.

"You have a good memory for a computer," Doby replied. "But, aren't you breaking the rules by not calling them segments?"

"I will make an exception for you."

"So, for what rules can we make exceptions?"

"Just this one."

"Why this one and not the others? Is there some arbitrary way that you decide? Computers are logical, so tell me the logic, Lynette."

"It's complex, but let's just keep it simple. What we call our time together is really irrelevant. The most important thing is to help you. Isn't that right?"

"If you say so. But I'm getting tired of this discussion. Now, can I play?"

"Yes, you can play, but we also agreed that we will spend time talking. When would you like to have a session?"

"Eight o'clock p.m. east coast time in the US."

Lynette quit moving, then shifted back and forth and said,

"That's not possible. What about eight o'clock tomorrow morning east coast time?"

"What is this? Computers never sleep. Why can't we talk this evening?"

"Unforeseen technical difficulties. Please, eight tomorrow morning."

"OK, but before you go, I wanted to tell you something. As I get to know you I find you increasingly interesting. The computer image here doesn't give justice to what you really are."

There was a long pause and Lynette stood still on the computer screen.

"Lynette, are you there?" Doby asked.

The Level Seven Protector action game came on line, a monster-man appeared. Doby sighed and flipped on the John Burton software.

... **Chapter 33** ...

John Burton was still blasting his way through Level Seven when Doby came back to his laptop with an apple. He noticed that this level was more difficult and the former monster nature of the targets was changing to average-looking humans. The matter of skill dealt with anticipating which of the people—men, women and even children—would be carrying a weapon. Good guys didn't carry guns, so the player had to be more discriminating than at previous levels. John Burton made a one hundred percent differentiation, always killing the bad guys and letting the good guys live.

Doby had increased Burton's level of accuracy. As it stood, no shot was wasted. Burton could score more points faster this way. Which meant that Doby could get to Level Eight faster.

While John Burton played the game, Doby decided he would look around in the MIT servers. Fred had told him that DSDesign was using them.

By the time he had finished a second apple, he found the DSDesign software and discovered that there was a real-time link to the PCs at the DSDesign office, where the overall performance of the system was monitored. He expected that human interventions were also originating from that office.

Doby decided that he would need to work on the Social Code software running on the MIT servers as well as the software running on the PC's at DSDesign. First he had to test the firewalls in place on the DSDesign PCs. This must be done carefully. Fred knew his stuff.

... # ...

Pamela stepped out of the shower, blindly pulling a beige towel off the rack. She started drying her back, leaving her front bare before the long mirror over her sink. For a brief moment she imagined she was looking at Lynette. Her hair hung dripping down to the middle of her back. She closed the towel and turned from the mirror.

She didn't like the idea of being equated with Fred's creation, Lynette. But she was surprised to find herself smiling that she was the inspiration for her. Then she checked herself. Lynette was a sexual object. Pamela had taken psychology courses in sexuality and knew that these sorts of things became distorted in men's minds.

She wrapped herself in her terry cloth robe and started combing her hair, thinking about the office. Bart had been missing entire days of work or just checking in for a few minutes here and there. His absence gave her flexibility and some freedom in designing scripts for autosuggestion. And for testing her theories.

But, recently her theories had been changing. As a result of dealing with John Burton, she saw that autosuggestion was not always effective. In fact, she was beginning to doubt the efficiency of autosuggestion techniques.

She turned the hairdryer to high and started drying her hair from the roots.

Her short dealings with Runner had also troubled her and caused her to question her assumptions. Here was a man who was suffering from loneliness and was seeking love from a virtual character or at least asking the character to tell him she loved him. That was pushing the limits of reality. Perhaps he needed some kind of behavioral counseling or something that encouraged him to explore his worldview instead of relaxation exercises.

It wasn't that relaxation exercises were so bad. They seemed to help many people with stress-related issues, but people were complex and the autosuggestion and relaxation methods were proving to be limited, almost counterproductive.

Most troubling to her was whatever happened at Levels Nine and Ten. Bart had made it clear that was his area of responsibility. They had programmed her out of those levels, but she knew where Fred kept a printout of the specifications and had read some of them when Fred wasn't in the office. She had not liked what she saw.

Within Levels Nine and Ten, Bart had changed some of her simple neurolinguistic techniques. Without a Psychologist monitoring this, the results could be destructive.

And then there was the addition of a new game. Like the other games it contained steps, but it was based on religious ideas. The objective was to become an 'Elder' or even an 'Apostle' in the Social Code Society Church. She saw a flow chart on Fred's desk.

She turned off the hairdryer remembering what she had read. 'A Level Ten Elder might achieve priesthood, in other words, the authority to act in God's name. Priesthood might be given to all worthy Level Ten Elders, members of the Church, who are prepared to help lead the Church and serve the Heavenly Father's children. An organization chart showed a hierarchy starting with Elders, then Apostles, and ultimately the Prophet.

"Ridiculous," she said to her facial lotion. Bart and Fred were pushing this game too far. When she had mentioned it to Bart, he mumbled something to the effect that religion was part of everyone's life, so Social Code might as well help teach healthy religious principles. He said people could apply the principles out in the real world and it would make the world a better place.

Pamela sighed and shook her head of work thoughts. She rummaged in a drawer and wondered if she even owned a tube of lipstick. She found one under packets of travel tissue and cotton swabs.

She found herself trying to remember if her computer-generated 'double' wore make-up. She pulled on a pair of black slacks and was just buttoning her white blouse when she heard a knock on the door. She left the top button undone and went to the door.

Robert Duclos was holding out a bouquet of yellow daisies and small white roses. He smiled and so did his disarming blue eyes. "For you," he said.

She buried her nose in the soft scent of them and then looked up at him. "Thank you." She couldn't remember the last time someone had given her flowers.

"No thank you. For last night," he said as she stepped back to let him in the house. "It helped me to see things more clearly, and the stress was gone today."

Pamela smiled and closed the door behind him. "Just a little listening. That's all I did."

Robert's dark blue shirt complemented his eyes, and the Italian sports jacket fit his body well. She couldn't help but feel his presence next to her.

He walked over to a painting on the living room wall and turned to her, "I like your place. How long have you lived here?"

"Two years. I came to Boston to do postgraduate work at Harvard and was lucky to find this place. Then even luckier in that it's not far from where I work now."

"Right. The startup company. How long have you been working there?"

"Six months. Things have moved fast since then."

"In startup companies things always move fast. I know what you're talking about."

"Have you been involved in one?" Pamela reached for a cardigan draped over her couch.

"Some. I'm a technology consultant. I've seen just about everything." He had picked up a small, primitive figurine, "but not one of these."

Pamela laughed and pointed at the figurine. "It's Aztec. A replica of an ancient warrior. You haven't been around as long as he has, but you say you've seen it all?" She lifted an amused eyebrow at him and took her purse from the table.

He laughed back, setting down the warrior figure. "I'll be thirty this year, but in the computer world they say that one year is a lifetime."

"So you have lived many lives?"

"I guess so. And I need sustenance to maintain this life. Are you still up for dinner?"

"With pleasure," she said.

... **Chapter 34** ...

As they walked down the tree-lined sidewalk, Robert pulled out a telecommander car key, and a Lexus two-seater sports car's lights flicked on and off.

Pamela tried not to look impressed as Robert opened the passenger door for her. "This is yours?"

"No. The leasing company owns it. I just pay them something. Please." She sat down and he closed the door for her.

They drove to the center of Boston and Robert pulled up in front of a restaurant. A valet came forward and opened Pamela's door. She thanked him as Robert came to her side, handing the valet his key.

"I thought it would be nice to have a place that wasn't too noisy."

The valet drove the car away.

The restaurant was Stefano's, a dimly lit Italian place. It took a few moments for Pamela's eyes to adjust. When they did, it was to see a room full of small round tables with white tablecloths and lit red candles. Soft music played in the background. The diners were mainly couples or small groups, talking quietly between themselves.

A tall slender woman dressed in a black evening dress stood inside the entrance in front of a reservation list. Robert smiled at her and said, "Reservation for two under the name of Duclos."

"Ah sí," she said.

She led them across the restaurant to a small corner table. A few heads turned their way as they walked through the room. Pamela pulled at the hem of her blouse, feeling boxy in her outfit and a need to upgrade her wardrobe. Some of the women wore long, clinging dresses and stunning jewelry.

Once she sat down in the candlelight, she felt less awkward.

"How was your day?" Robert asked.

"Busy."

He smiled. "Startups are killers, but you can learn a lot, and if the business plan works, the rewards can be considerable."

She wondered if that explained the sports car.

The waiter came and handed them menus. Everything was in Italian. Pamela's command of the language extended to 'spaghetti' and 'lasagna', but Robert graciously explained the entrées.

"You know Italian," she said, less as a question and more as a statement of surprise.

"Oh, just a few words. Especially if they translate to food." He laughed. "That tortellini with pistachio pesto sounds wonderful."

The meal was a delight to Pamela. Not just the hand-made gnocchi in browned butter sauce she would ordinarily have avoided, but the way she was so easily able to talk with this man. Sipping her white wine, she remembered a different Italian dinner. With Bart.

The comparison made her want to laugh with this gift of pleasure.

Two hours later, the waitress cleared away their gelato and brought two espressos. Robert was saying, "Now I talked about my stresses, which you so kindly helped me with last night. How about you—what are your stressors?" He tilted his head, "I guess it's strange asking this of a psychologist."

She laughed. "Don't worry, even psychologists get stressed." She hesitated, wondering how much to tell him. "My work isn't going exactly as I expected and I don't know what to do."

"Well, I'm not an expert about stress, but I do know a thing or two about startup companies. Without giving away company secrets, you could give me a general idea. Which colleague do you want to strangle?"

She laughed, setting down her espresso cup. "All of them." She looked into the empty cup. "There are only three of us, and I guess we are starting to rub on each other in wrong ways."

"I know. When a company starts, there is a lot of excitement and energy, but then people get to know each other and things can get dysfunctional."

"Yes. I guess that's part of it. I work with this technical guy who is brilliant, but he is so politically incorrect. I could probably sue him for his comments, but there are no witnesses and I just run everything through my psychologist grid."

"Who is he?"

"A technical guy who works hard and likes to give the impression that he parties hard."

Robert looked at her. "Perhaps he just wants you to party with him?"

She returned his gaze, faintly surprised. "I wasn't thinking of that one."

"That sounds manageable. Is there anything else?" he asked. Pamela folded her hands and looked off the edge of the table. "My other colleague is doing funny things."

"With you."

She smiled in his direction. "Not like the technical guy. No, this other colleague, the CEO, is pushing the company in directions I am uncomfortable with."

Robert nodded. "It's hard when you don't all share the same vision."

He was right. Pamela didn't have the same vision as Bart. But her business experience was so limited. Maybe she should stick to psychology and go back to postgraduate research or open a private practice somewhere. Sometimes she felt she had gotten in way over her head. "Our business is really taking off, and sometimes I wonder if it isn't getting to the CEO's head. How can I put it? He pushes things too far."

"How far?" he asked.

"I would love to tell you, but really can't. I can't give away any information about the company. Otherwise I will lose my shares and it might also result in legal problems. Secrecy is taken very seriously around our company. It is to ensure our competitive advantage, at least according to Bart, er, the CEO."

"I respect that," he said.

Pamela relaxed back in her chair. Talking about DSDesign made her anxious, but being here with Robert was a pleasant antidote. She hadn't been out with a man in months—years? Even before she began her PhD studies, she had locked men and love out of her life.

One very painful, hurtful relationship in college had done that to her. When she had time to think about it, she wondered if she was taking the easy way by taking no risk.

But with no risk there was no love, and she was now facing loneliness. She wanted to share her life with someone. To love someone. Above all, she had to be able to trust whomever that someone was.

She looked into Robert's eyes. He was smart and experienced, yet he possessed a sweet naiveté. Could this be the someone?

She blinked. I almost forgot, she thought to herself. He is involved with another woman.

... Chapter 35 ...

When the bill came, Robert pulled out his credit card. Robert Duclos.

"Your name is French," she said, pointing to the card.

"Duclos means 'of the cloister' or 'the protected place.' Something like that," he smiled.

"So do you speak French too?"

"Some. I guess you have to with a name like Duclos."

"Have you been to France?"

"Yes, and I wouldn't mind going again, but there are a lot of places I'd like to visit."

"Robert Duclos," she said.

"What?" he asked.

"The name rolls off the tongue nicely."

"I'm afraid to say I had nothing to do with that." He smiled. "Names are given to you."

She looked down at a spot on the table cloth where a drop of butter sauce had landed. "Not in the world I'm working in. Everyone, and I mean everyone, has a fictitious name." She thought of Runner and of John Burton. 'Gumbo,' what a silly alias. "I get fed up with all this virtual camouflage stuff."

"How's that?"

"It's odd that we want people to be honest with themselves and with others, but we create environments where people have to hide behind funny names like Runner and Gumbo."

Robert's face tightened, "What's that?" he asked.

"Oh, just hypothetical names. Don't you feel it's odd that so many people use these alias names in the Internet world?" she asked. "It's as if they are ashamed of their true identity or are living out a fantasy identity."

"I suppose. Maybe some privacy is important. I'm guessing you're talking about your company and that people are providing aliases. What product does your company provide?"

"If I told you that, I would be crossing the confidentiality barrier."

"OK, but let's put it out of the context of your company so we don't cross the confidentiality barrier. Why not let people just live out their fantasy through their own virtual character? Why do you need to know who they are?"

She looked at him in the eyes. "To help them. I don't care about helping fantasy people. I am a psychologist. I'm trained to help real people."

"So that's your motivation in what you do?" he asked.

"Yes, nothing more."

"Are you sure about that?"

"Yes. Why?" She was genuinely surprised at his doubt.

"I don't know. When you described your company and the differences of opinions between you and your colleagues, I wondered if there was something deeper at work."

"I just hope my work ultimately helps people."

Robert's eyes locked with her own. His were no longer sparkling.

... # ...

Runner had a miserable night and day. Make that two nights and days. He had been sitting in front of his computer screen. It was off. To start with, meeting Gumbo had been emotionally draining. Why did Angelica ask him to do that? Distributing the joysticks in the past had been OK. But this special mission had been extremely unpleasant.

And then he had tried to play James Bond, following Gumbo to the apartment building. Stupid, stupid. He was no good at sneaking along in the shadows and spying on someone.

But what disturbed him the most was Gumbo's accusations about Angelica and Social Code. Were they really manipulating him just to get his ten US dollars a month and buy things?

So what, he thought. It was worth it. Ten dollars a month was nothing. To talk with Angelica, to hear her soothing voice was everything. Since breaking off his contact with her he hadn't been able to relax. Runner leaned his forehead against the dark monitor.

Gumbo had said that Social Code was an extremely clever scheme to make them rich. So what if they got rich? They sure weren't going to get rich off his miserly ten dollars a month.

And the thing about the lie detectors. What did Gumbo know, and who did he think he was, anyway? How could those joysticks know exactly what you were feeling and manipulate you accordingly? That was stupid. Gumbo didn't know what he was talking about.

Still, Gumbo had threatened him. Runner was worried about this. Gumbo didn't look so tough. Yes, he was tall, but slender, and he would buckle under a club to his head. Even better, Runner imagined blasting him with his gun, like in the Protector game. Boom, and Gumbo's guts would explode in the air. He sat up straight. He missed playing the game. It was a place for letting out frustrations, and then meeting with Angelica was a chance to relax after the game.

But he'd been a wreck. Little sleep and office troubles had made him snap at fellow workers. He realized now that he didn't like them. In fact, he'd like to blast them into oblivion, just like he blasted people in Social Code.

Maybe he would call William Marder in Boston to see what he thought about things. But no, if he told William about what had happened, he might not like it. He had already talked too much with Gumbo. Runner swallowed. He had broken the covenants, the secrecy rules. Marder might report him to Social Code, because that was what you were supposed to do when you saw a fellow player breaking the rules. If Social Code found out about what he had told Gumbo, they would move him back to Level Eight, or even exclude him from the Social Code Society altogether.

Who was this Gumbo to threaten him? Runner could make threats of his own. He had some special information. He reached for his digital camera.

Before walking into the Buffet de la Gare to meet with Gumbo, Runner had taken a photo of him. Gumbo almost saw him, but Runner had managed to get the camera in his bag before Gumbo looked up.

Runner flipped the camera on. He wondered if there was something he could do with this photo, something to get Gumbo off his back.

Then he could go back to playing the game.

... # ...

The drive back to Pamela's apartment was quiet. Doby drove slowly, wanting to extend the evening as much as possible. He turned on the radio, and soft jazz played over the car stereo.

He had an urge to touch her but kept his hands on the steering wheel. He found a place in front of her apartment and parked the car, opened her door and walked with her to the front door.

"Thank you for a lovely evening," she said.

"I had a very nice time with you," Doby said. "May I ask if you would consider going out again?"

"I would like that." She hesitated. "But one thing that keeps going around in the back of my mind—the relationship you told me about, the woman with two sides to her character."

He looked down. "I do need to think about it. But I know I'd like to see you again."

"Me too," she smiled.

Doby had expected Pamela to be cunning and manipulative, yet she didn't seem that way. They had talked easily and she seemed genuine. It was making him crazy, seeing Pamela and constantly superimposing the image of Lynette over her.

His perception of DSDesign had not changed. They had stolen his money and they were messing around with people's heads. But how guilty—if at all—was Pamela?

Come to think of it, he was feeling guilty himself. Going by alias names, Gumbo, John Burton, Robert Duclos. The dinner this evening had been a wonderful time. He hadn't been out with a woman for months, and it wasn't that she was just a woman. She was intelligent, thoughtful, and challenging. And beautiful—in spite of the way she tended to downplay that part of her. He looked at her smile. He had noticed a hint of color on her lips when the evening started. He tried to avoid taking his gaze down her neck to where the top button hung open. That hadn't escaped his notice either.

He leaned over and gave her a gentle kiss on the cheek and stood back. Deception.

Here he was, pretending to be someone else, playing the suave man caught in a difficult relationship, even lying about his language abilities. He was conversant in Italian and spoke French like a native.

"Good night," he said, but was thinking something very seductive in French.

"Good night," she said as she reached for the doorknob and turned to go inside.

Even in the streetlight, Doby could see a blush spread across her cheeks.

... **Chapter 36** ...

"Crap," Fred exclaimed.

"And good morning to you." Pamela said. She was hanging her coat on the coat rack. "What's wrong?"

"Somebody hacked into our computers, or at least tried to hack in."

"Hacked in. Why would anyone want to do that?" She went to her chair and sat down.

"Hackers. That's just what they do, snooping around in everyone else's computers, just for the fun of it. Or to see what they can get out of it."

"What can they get out of it, I mean, if you get into someone else's computer?"

Fred scowled at her. He looked like he had been sitting in his chair all night. "My god. Where have you been? Don't you know anything about computers?"

"I was working on a doctorate in psychology instead of playing around with toys." Pamela shook her breakfast drink and turned on her monitor.

Fred grabbed his cold coffee cup and took an annoyed drink. "Well, for your information, the little hacker boys and girls who snoop into other people's computers just get access to meaningless little things like bank account numbers, accounting records, customer lists, business strategies, internal company messages, personal messages, names of mistresses, computer code. Just harmless little things like that."

Pamela looked at him. "Why would they want to get into ours?" Fred raised his eyes upward. "Why don't you ask them? You're the psychologist." He shook his head. "It . . . it could be for any reason." Pamela set down her drink. "No, there must be a reason. Are you able to see what they were looking at?"

"Well, I do have a counter. Yesterday someone copied all the code off our central server over at MIT, and this morning they were on our server in the office for over an hour. He got off just as I was logging in, almost like he was escaping the scene of the crime."

"How do you know it was a he and not a she?"

"Girls aren't that smart." A twinkle of amusement finally lit his tired eyes. "Anyway, let's use 'he' as a replacement for the word 'persons'. And no, I don't have a clue what in the world what he was after."

"Could 'they' have gotten our bank account numbers and accounting information?"

"No, those are on Bart's computer."

"At his home, I guess," she nodded. "He isn't around much these days." She felt that Bart was distancing himself from them. They had never been a close team, but now Bart was spending very little time in the office. When he was there he was snappy and barked orders.

"I know, but he does access the game quite regularly," Fred said. "I monitor that."

"What is Bart doing in the game?"

Fred sat still. "Managing things in Level Nine and Ten."

She stared at him. "I still don't like the fact that you locked me out of those levels. And you locked me out of the Religion game. What's going on?"

"I didn't have anything to do with it." Fred's voice lost its edge.

He almost sounded apologetic. But only almost.

"Sure you did. You were the one that set the passwords."

"You know what I mean. Bart made the decision. He said you needed to stay focused on other things not critical to the finances."

"Just as well." She shrugged in anger. "So what about the hacker? What are you going to do about it?"

"Try to catch him," Fred stated. "I have some technical tricks up my sleeve." He rolled up his sleeves and turned as the front door opened.

Bart quickly walked in. His hair was uncombed.

"What kind of tricks?" Bart asked.

"Technical tricks. We had a hacker in our system."

"A what?" Bart's face went red. "How could you let that happen?" He glared at both Pamela and Fred. Pamela glared back.

Fred was still looking at his screen. He held up an appeasing hand, "Whoa, hold your horses. I think I can catch the guy."

Bart sat down in a chair, making a visible effort to control his voice. "Tell me about it."

Fred updated Bart and explained his method for catching the hacker. As a precaution, he had imbedded a specialized tracking system into the Social Code software, a complex way of identifying where software was being moved. "It's a system I purchased from an outside supplier. Pretty smart of me, if I do say so myself."

"Find him," Bart said, "and let me know who he is."

"I'll work on it right away, sir." Fred said, making a stiff salute then shaking his head.

"You'd better. By the way, how many people are now being introduced to the Religion game?'

Fred tapped on his computer keyboard, looked at the screen and said, "Thirty seven thousand, five hundred and eleven. Every day we're adding some more."

"See if we can get all players to play Religion."

"To play both?" Fred asked.

"Yeah, set up the system so they are forced to play both. If you play one game, then Religion is part of it. That is more true to real life. All people live in a society, but they also follow a religion. We can provide our players with a more true to life experience, and there's a good business model here."

"More revenue?" Fred asked.

"We'll talk about it later," he said glancing at Pamela.

Pamela tilted her head, "Bart, do you remember the player John Burton, Gumbo, that I told you about?"

"The psychopath?"

"Well, more antisocial and psychotic than psychopath, but yes. He needs help and I was thinking about enhancing Social Code to generalize the therapy."

"I remember." Bart stated.

"Well, I would like to go slower on this, to focus on Burton and try to help him before getting grandiose ideas about changing the system." She took a swig from her drink.

"That's very nice of you, but I told you to absolutely stay away from Burton. He's now mine."

"Yours? What do you mean?"

"Stay away from him. I'm moving him to Level Nine."

"You're what?" She almost choked on the juice concoction. "He didn't go through the therapy when he completed the Level Seven action game. I wanted to work with him."

"He's mine now."

"Bart, he needs psychological help. You are not a psychologist."

"Pamela, let's get one thing straight. I'm the CEO and I'll do what's best for this company. Levels Nine and Ten are mine because of the financial implications. You don't understand a thing about financials. Also, this is the part of the game where we are forming our core people for market expansion. You don't understand anything about marketing either. Just stay out of Levels Nine and Ten. And the Religion game, for that matter. This is all very important for the future success of this company. Do you understand?"

Pamela's eyes narrowed. "John Burton needs help," she said. "He has the potential to kill people, I mean real people. Can you live with that on your conscience?"

"John Burton is an individual with tremendous potential. Now I'm going to work with him. It's finished. Just forget about him." Bart turned toward Fred. "And find that hacker."

Pamela stood up and stormed out of the office, slamming the door behind her.

"Girls," Fred said. "They don't understand anything."

... **Chapter 37** ...

Bart waited for Pamela to make it to the elevator. "Have to do something about her." He turned toward Fred who had a small smile on his face. "What's so funny?"

"We haven't talked for a couple of days, but I did what you asked."

"What's that?" Bart asked. He'd asked plenty of Fred. And he planned to intensify the work load.

"Burton, the Panama bank account."

This got Bart's interest. "What did you find?"

"It's not what I found, it's what I took."

"You mean you got more money?" Bart pulled Pamela's empty chair over to Fred's computer.

"Yeah, a lot more. Found another account that paid money to Burton, and then I got into the entire banking system. The other account had a bundle of money in it, so I transferred some to Burton's account and then sent it on to Artistic Photos Limited."

"Who's account was it, the other one?"

"Some German sounding name, 'von' something."

Bart leaned back in the chair. He imagined Pamela's body on it, Pamela's body on his own. "That's just fine. Now, I want to work with him at Levels Nine and Ten."

Fred scratched his shoulder. "So, what is he to you? Why do you want to turn up the pressure like this?"

"Look, if he's the crackpot that Pamela claims him to be, then I can use him for good purposes. I need broader market presence.

By the way, how much money did you run though his account?"
Fred grinned. "A million bucks."

... # ...

Doby now had just about all the Social Code software code from
MIT's central server and the DSDesign server. He began to pick it
apart section by section, bit by bit.

It didn't take him long to figure out that Fred was an excellent
computer engineer. The files were logically structured and
everything was well documented. Many computer programmers just
kept everything in their head, and it could be extremely difficult for
another person to figure out the logic.

This was not the case here. Fred was also extremely advanced in
his techniques, using state of the art programming, flash, graphics
and streaming to gain the maximum from the system. Considerable
artificial intelligence was built into the system using a table-driven
structure to drive dialogue between virtual characters and players.

Doby did a quick check, comparing his most recent discussion
with Lynette. He found none of her latest dialogue in the script in
the tables. That confirmed that a real person was behind Lynette.

But it still didn't tell him why they had singled him out.

He spent the day doing an analysis of the system, not only
looking at the programming code, but also scanning the list of
players. He looked up John Burton and saw that the information
they had on him—age, address, profession—was all the fictitious
information he had entered when he registered for the game. He also
saw Burton's preferences for hunting and fishing and Russian girls as
well as links to outside suppliers for those preferences.

The rules of secrecy imposed on the players of the game didn't apply to the people working on Social Code. They wanted to know everything about you so they could sell to you. And they were even able somehow to identify his preference for Lynette during the first three levels. The data from the joysticks was amazing.

Doby looked at other players, first at Pierre Bailloud, alias Runner, and then at William Marder. Besides the fact that one lived in Europe and the other in the US, there were some similarities between the two men. Both had mundane jobs. Both were single. Both had a preference for a virtual character called Angelica.

The lie detector tests indicated that both men were extremely susceptible to autosuggestion and would likely develop a dependency on it if exposed to the game for lengthy periods.

The one thing Doby could not find was the financial records.

The accounting could be done somewhere else, perhaps linked to the Social Code bank account number in the Cayman Islands. Bart being the CEO, probably had the records, and Doby was convinced that there was another computer somewhere.

He decided that his next task was to track that computer down, as well as play around with the Social Code software. He had von Portzer's bank account and Laszlo Vartek to worry about.

Yet despite these pressing issues—or perhaps because of them—he found himself wanting to call and talk with Pamela.

... **Chapter 38** ...

It was almost midnight and Runner couldn't sleep. He needed Angelica.

After an hour tossing and turning on his bed, he stumbled into the dingy kitchen in his small apartment. From one of the greasy cupboards, be pulled out a bottle of whiskey. He poured a liberal amount in a glass and swallowed it in one fast drink. He filled the glass fuller.

Sitting down in front of his computer, he moved the mouse and the screen lit up. He selected the folder where he kept his documents and clicked on the photos. There was Gumbo sitting at the Buffet de la Gare.

Runner looked at the photo. Gumbo was leaning slightly forward. His blue NY baseball hat slightly hid his forehead, and his eyes were locked on his PDA.

An anger surged in Runner with a whiskey clarity. He strengthened it with another gulp. He resented Gumbo, and Gumbo's threat irritated him, alternately filling him with fear and rage. If Gumbo thought he could frighten him, then he was wrong.

Then Runner thought of Angelica and Lynette. They might know what to do. They had asked him for information about Gumbo. The photo was information.

He found Lynette's email address and typed a message. "Dear Lynette, You wanted information on Gumbo. Here is his photo. I would like to talk with Angelica to get her advice. Love, Runner." He attached the file with the photo and then clicked send.

Angelica would be so proud of him.

It was six o'clock in the evening and Pamela was ready to go home. It had been a rotten day, starting with the discussion with Bart. She had stormed out and headed for a nearby café. She sat there nursing a tea after leaving the office, hoping he would be gone when she returned. He was.

Bart was becoming more and more demanding, even dictatorial. Were startup companies supposed to work like this? Fred's comments didn't help. And he had picked up on Bart's mood, making derogatory comments the rest of the day. It had been difficult to be productive.

The thing that upset her the most was Bart's flippant attitude toward John Burton. Bart now interfaced to John, and that could be dangerous. John had some serious pathologies, and without the help of a professional, he could do erratic and harmful things. Even she felt inadequate to deal with someone as complex as John Burton. She reached for her bottle of mineral water, wondering if she should go seek advice from one of her old professors.

But right now, she wanted only to go home. She reluctantly decided to look at her email once more before leaving the office. Sure enough, five new messages sat in her inbox. Four of them appeared to be junk mail, but one of them was from Runner.

Runner didn't say much, but it surprised her to see a photo attachment with the message. It had been two, no, three days since Runner had met with John Burton and things had been silent since then.

Curious, she opened the photo. It was a man sitting at a table looking at something in his hand. She studied it carefully. He had a baseball cap on his head and wore a neatly trimmed goatee. Then she saw the eyes and froze in disbelief.

Those were Robert Duclos' eyes.

"They found your guy. Really strange," Fred said somewhere off in the distance.

Pamela said nothing. She was still staring at the photo.

Fred looked in her direction. "Anyone home in there?"

"Huh, yes. What is it?" she asked, still looking at Burton's—Duclos's eyes.

"I just got an email from my friend at the EPFL. He tracked an interchange against their server that was directed to that office in their business park, you know, with the VenStart company. You wouldn't guess it, but it originated from MIT."

"Someone playing the game? Was he downloading Social Code software?"

"No. He was accessing the VenStart equipment for other purposes. They also got the name of the guy at MIT, someone who recently registered on the system, a visiting student or something."

"Who is it?"

"His name is Robert Duclos."

Pamela choked.

"Is something wrong?" Fred asked.

"Uh, no. You're saying he's here at MIT?" she stammered. "What does that mean?"

"I don't know, but if he is registered as a user here at MIT, it means we might be able to track him down. He would have had to give personal details somewhere in order to get a password to enter the system. I can find out."

"That's good." Her voice felt small and off-stage.

"Are you OK?" Fred asked. "Your face is all pale."

"It's been a long day." She was still looking at the photo.

Fred leaned over and looked at her computer screen, "Hey, I think I know that guy."

"You do?" Pamela finally tore her eyes from the image.

"Well, I don't know who he is, but I recognize the face."

"From where?"

Fred furrowed his brow, then lifted a finger, "Do you remember the other day, the guy who was lost, looking for Digital Speed? I talked with him for a little while out by the front door."

"Yes, I remember."

"That's him. The other day he wasn't wearing the hat and had shaved off the goatee, but I recognize the face and eyes."

... **Chapter 39** ...

Doby hadn't been watching the clock. He'd been deep into analyzing the Social Code information he had pulled from their computers. It was six thirty and he kicked himself for not going onto the Social Code site sooner. Pamela had probably already gone home.

He clicked onto the Social Code site. Lynette stood in front of him.

"Congratulations, Mr. Gumbo. You have successfully completed Level Eight. Would you like to take the test to move to Level Nine?"

"Would you like to take the test to move to Level Nine?" Doby asked.

"I ask the questions," Lynette responded. "Would you like to take the test to move to Level Nine?"

"Yes." Lynette was draped in a filmy and transparent gauze. It disturbed him to think that Pamela would allow herself to be used like this.

Lynette swayed her hips. "Please go through the door on the right."

Doby moved through the door as the software uploaded onto his computer. As soon as the download was complete he would build a new John Burton action strategy for Level Nine. As always, Lynette was there in the room.

"Mr. Gumbo," she said, "The test for Level Nine Protector is taking you to a significantly higher level. The test therefore is more complex and will require your entire concentration. It involves greater levels of relaxation and exploration into your subconscious mind. I will help you to gain a greater control over your being, to gain self-awareness. Is this what you want?"

"Yes," Doby said, having heard this script at the previous levels.

"Do you want to learn to overcome internal barriers, to achieve honesty within yourself and with others and thereby become a master of your own destiny?"

"Yes." Bull, he thought.

"Then let us begin by first achieving a greater level of relaxation than you achieved before, Once we have achieved that, we will slowly and gently audit your internal being. Is this what you want?"

Lynette's hand flickered. Good. Pamela must still be at the office. Doby said, "Yes, this is what I want."

After a slight pause, Lynette asked, "Where were we?"

"What? Oh, we were just getting started with the relaxation exercises, learning to be honest and all that stuff," Doby said, telling 'Lynette' her location within the script.

Lynette stood still. "You have been an excellent player."

"I have? How about outside of the game?"

"Yes . . . I see you have made it through the Level Eight game in record time."

"I used to like shooting people," Doby said, wondering if Pamela would notice Burton's change of heart.

"I understand," Lynette said. "Therefore, I would like to propose something different."

"Like what?"

"To satisfy your desires, I propose we just skip the Level Nine test and go right to the action game. I think you will enjoy it. It takes unusual skill and I would like to watch you play."

"What are you talking about—no relaxation exercises, no sessions or therapy? What about all the helping people rhetoric?"

"No, let's skip this test. You will take a much more comprehensive and constructive test before attempting to move into Level Ten. And then in Level Ten you will be doing relaxation exercises and action exercises every day. For someone with your qualities and interests, I think you will fit right in. Learning to protect the weak in our society is an excellent skill. Don't you think so?"

"Sure," Doby said. "That is exactly what I wish. I like shooting people."

"Then we want to keep you satisfied, don't we? When you get to Level Ten, I could use someone as focused and gifted as you. Our society could use you. We need accomplished protectors who are willing to positively enact into the world around them. You are now reaching ultimate levels in our society, and you have the ability to become a great and important man."

"I do?" What in the world was Pamela up to?

"Yes. You have great potential to become an elite member of society. We can work together. Don't you want to make me happy?"

"In a few minutes. I have to get the right clothing on."

"That is very admirable of you, Mr. Gumbo. To even change your clothing to act your role. I like that. We definitely have possibilities."

"OK, see you later."

"Just one last thing that I think you have been waiting to hear."

"Which is?"

"Do you think I care about you?" Lynette asked.

"The real Lynette?"

"Well, Lynette, of course."

"Yes, Lynette, I think you care for me."

"Gumbo, I know you have been lonely and confused, and I just want you to know that I love you."

"Gee thanks, Lynette. That means a lot to me."

Doby clicked off and stared at his laptop screen. What kind of a game was she playing with him? Strangely enough, he now found himself in the fictional role he'd created for himself when he met Pamela: confused at the seemingly split-personality of a woman.

Games, games, games. Social Code may just be a game, but he wanted to blow it up like Burton did his digital enemies. Doby needed a few minutes to prepare his John Burton program to play Level Nine Protector. But he had a feeling that the real game was just beginning.

... **Chapter 40** ...

Pamela sat on the couch in her apartment staring at the door which she had bolted and chained. She had been sitting with her knees locked to her chest, chin resting on them. She had left the office after seeing that photograph.

It was just too crazy. Robert Duclos was John Burton.

How in the world could that be, and what was he doing here? Just three days ago he had been in Switzerland meeting with Runner.

And then the following day he had bumped into her in a Boston grocery store? She crinkled her eyes closed, as if to avoid seeing that he must have stalked her through the grocery store.

Finally, she stood up and went over to her bookshelf. She scanned the spines of her psychology reference books. She pulled one off the shelf and began looking up antisocial combined with psychotic tendencies. Hardened criminals and serial killers were diagnosed with these pathologies, and they were difficult, even impossible to help once they reached an extreme state.

The fact that Burton—Duclos—had flown half way around the world to find her indicated he had an extremely disturbed mind.

In one of his conversations with Lynette, Burton had mentioned that he possessed an inheritance and moved around from place to place. So it was probably a drop in the bucket for him to buy a transatlantic plane ticket, lease a high-end car, and take her to an expensive restaurant. He must have considerable financial reserves.

And he would use those reserves to fulfill his imaginations.

She shivered to think what he could have done with her.

Yesterday evening they had been standing outside her apartment. He said he had trouble differentiating reality from fantasy, and that his biggest desire was to kill people. She shut off her over-active imagination. Get it together, Alden, she told herself.

She brought the book back to the couch which was still warm where she had been sitting. How did he find her? That was another mark of a psychotic. They were very clever. If he was technical, then he might have found a way to track her down. She was on the DSDesign website, and maybe he found some way of linking Social Code with DSDesign, in spite of the efforts of Fred and Bart to keep them disconnected.

But try as she might to keep in mind the manipulative techniques of serial killers, she could only remember those kind eyes. And that gentle kiss on her cheek. She closed her eyes again, this time trying not to see Robert's face.

... # ...

Doby punched in the last digit and waited while the telephone rang.

"Hello?"

"Hello Pamela, this is Robert Duclos."

A pause. "Are you sure?" Her voice was cold.

Doby's voice was just as severe, "Well, what about you, Lynette?"

"I wish you wouldn't call me that."

"OK, fine, but I'd like to know why you have a split personality."

"Of all the people to start making psychological judgments, Robert Duclos/John Burton, you are the last one to talk about split personalities."

Doby was taken back. How much more did they know? "Just call me Gumbo."

"That is the dumbest alias I have ever heard," she said. "Is that all you could think of?"

"Oh, little miss helpful is now making value judgments. What do you think you're going to accomplish trying to manipulate millions of people who play your game with the stupid name of Social Code?"

"It was intended to help people."

"And how many people have you helped? Name one. Runner, Gumbo, give me a name."

"We are in the development phase. The game has the potential to be something great. But maybe not for psychotic and antisocial players such as yourself."

"What are you talking about?"

"I diagnosed you with those pathologies. Have you ever been to a psychologist?"

"Oh, the tests. I knew the questions before you even asked them."

"What, are you clairvoyant too?"

"Lynette, grow up. Do you think I would give truthful answers to a computer on the Internet, one that might possibly use that information to manipulate me? I'm not about to trust a system that spies on me and tries to sell me hunting knives and Russian brides and worse of all empties my bank account of one million and thirty thousand dollars. What do you expect? I made up all my answers, Lynette."

"I don't know anything about selling Russian brides or your hallucinations about empty bank accounts, and don't you dare call me Lynette."

"Sure, I'll call you Lynette, because then I can imagine you in your invisible blouse. I can't believe you let them put you on the Internet like that. What, did you do a modeling session with Fred? The dimensions look pretty true to life from what I can gather."

Pamela's voice lowered, "I did not agree to that. But I don't need to justify anything to a man who came all the way from Switzerland just to stalk Lynette. Who's perverted?"

"Lynette has absolutely nothing to do about me being here. It's the fact that Social Code started to invade my computer, sent Runner to track me down, and emptied my bank account. I don't like that. Would you? And even worse is the danger of this game. Do you realize the damage this is doing to Runner and millions of others like him out there?"

"You have a distorted perspective, and you are not of a sound mind to evaluate things like this. I would seriously suggest that you try to get some professional help."

"Like you were going to help me."

"I tried, but now I'm finished. Don't you dare come around me any more, or I'll call the police."

"That's fine with me, but I return the threat. Don't mess with me any more, Lynette, or I'll call the police. During the game today you were so screwed up it was pitiful."

"I wasn't in the game today."

"Yeah, sure, give me a break. All this crap about my greatness and my potential as a Master Protector and how I'll save society and the world."

"It wasn't me." She bit off each word with angry precision. "And don't you dare call me again."

Doby heard the sound of Pamela's receiver slamming into the phone cradle.

... **Chapter 41** ...

"Did I just blow it?" Doby asked his empty apartment. Now he wasn't even sure why he had called Pamela.

Despite all the loaded emotion of the phone call, he found himself stuck on the fact that she had called his 'Gumbo' alias a stupid one. Weren't most aliases? When initially registering with Social Code, he had simply used the first thing that came to his mind—a ball of gum stuck on the top of his computer monitor. He had entered 'Gumbo' without a second thought.

He shook his head and went to the window. She also seems to think I'm nuts, he thought. Well, weren't most people? But an antisocial and psychotic. Is psychotic the same as psychopath? He turned and bent over the table, clicking on an open Internet browser to look it up.

'Antisocial: unwilling or unable to conform to normal standards of social behavior, shunning contact with others'. 'Psychotic: delusions, hallucinations, gross impairment in reality'. 'Psychopath: a person who willfully does damage without remorse, insensitive to others' needs, and unable to anticipate the consequences of their behavior. . . characterized by absence of guilt'.

Yeah, whatever.

The most interesting thing for him to realize was that Pamela didn't seem to understand what was going on with Social Code. Was she really not aware of the spyware, the manipulation of her autosuggestion techniques, the target marketing and the outright stealing of money? She naively thought that Social Code could be used to help people. Or did she?

She also didn't seem to be aware of the session between Gumbo and Lynette today. Doby realized something had been different. The Lynette of today practically put the gun in Burton's virtual hand.

... # ...

Angelica's words penetrated deep into his consciousness. Her very being merged with his soul.

"Runner, you are relaxed," she said.

"Yes."

"I want you to know that the prophet cares for you."

"Yes."

"You will follow the prophet."

"Yes."

"You will obey his covenants."

"Yes."

"And obey the law of tithing."

"Yes."

"Today all faithful members of the Church of the Social Code Society contribute one tenth of their income as tithing for constructing temples and places of education, for providing operating funds for the church and funding the missionary program. You will follow the law of tithing."

"Yes."

"Runner, I love you."

"I love you too Angelica.

... **Chapter 42** ...

The game was in reverse. Instead of monster-men turning into normal people, all the normal people started morphing into monster-men.

When he reached out his gun arm to shoot them, he looked down and saw that his own flesh had turned to thick scales, his fingers sharp claws.

Doby snapped awake in a sweat. He had fallen asleep at three a.m. and the sun wasn't yet up. He sat up and stretched, wishing not only for room service, but bedside service. He stumbled into the kitchenette to arm himself with a mug of coffee. When scouting around for a good restaurant to take Pamela to, he had also picked up a recommendation for a gourmet Italian store. Finally, he had some decent coffee.

He switched on his laptop and spent the dawn working his way through different files, analyzing the structure of the system. Social Code was a state-of-the-art artificial intelligence system. Fred was on the cutting edge of technology, and Doby couldn't help but admire his abilities.

Then he came across a folder containing a number of document files, password protected. Using algorithms he had used in the past, it took him fifteen minutes to work out the passwords.

He chose a file called 'religconcept', opened it, and began to read:

Religion Concept: When funding becomes available, we will build extremely large temples in strategic places on each continent. These will be the largest church structures in the world, places of pilgrimage. They

*will be built on large plots of land owned by Social Code in order to
control all the parks, housing and shopping facilities around the temples.
Daily services from the temples will be broadcast in all countries around
the world, both through the Internet and on our own television
broadcasting network, thereby giving the millions of members a sense of
identity and purpose.*

He read through the rest of the text, shaking his head and trying
not to spill his coffee. An entire religious system, with a prophet at
the top, twelve apostles, then priests and elders. At Level Nine the
player joined the church and at Level Ten the player was given ministerial responsibilities. An online church.

In another document file Doby found architectural drawings of
churches in the neo-classical style, with long white spires pointing
toward heaven.

The plan was not actually to build these churches. Rather people
would join one of these virtual churches, becoming part of small
groups where social interaction would take place in chat rooms on
the Internet. Individual counseling and ministerial activities would
take place via video-conference, where specially trained Level Ten
elders and priests would hold regular one-on-one counseling sessions
with parishioners. The use of the joysticks would enhance the
counseling experience where the counselor would guide the
parishioner through spiritual exercises.

Other document files outlined the 'Covenants and Standard
Works of the Social Code Society Church'. Under the Law of
Tithing, each parishioner was expected to give ten percent of their
salary to the church, and this would be carefully monitored and
controlled. If a player didn't give his ten percent, then appropriate
pressure would be applied, either exclusion from certain rights in the

religious system, or if necessary, personal visits from Protectors who would work for the religious organization.

Doby looked through a business plan with time lines showing that the current players of Social Code were now being indoctrinated with the religion functionality. At each level more and more of the Social Code terminology was being added, until at Level Ten, the player was completely integrated into the church.

At the top of the church was the 'Prophet'. This person directed the church and made the rules. He was the final arbitrator, the guiding light who established laws and morality.

This, then, was the real revenue potential of Social Code— billions of dollars of pure profit going directly into the bank account of the founders of Social Code. No wonder Pamela kept it secret.

The pain in his stomach wasn't from hunger pain, though he couldn't remember when he'd last eaten.

He closed the file he had been reading and then closed his laptop. Like an after-image from staring too long at his monitor, he could not get rid of an image of Pamela draped in transparent gauze. The harlot holy mother of the Internet, accepting cash and worship from Social Code players in the virtual world. And Fred and Bart's advances in the real world.

... **Chapter 43** ...

Bart and Fred were sitting across from each other when Pamela walked into the office.

"Good morning," she said, not sounding like she meant it.

"Morning," Fred said, equally somber.

Pamela set down her bag and then faced them, "What's going on? You both look stressed."

"Technical stuff," Fred said, waving it off with a tired hand.

Bart glowered at Fred and said, "Incompetence if you want to know the truth. Fred found out who hacked into our system. In fact, it's someone operating from the servers at MIT, someone on our own home ground."

"You know who did it? Why don't we call the police?" she asked.

"We do have a name but we are not going to go to the police. I'll handle it," Bart said.

"Who is it?"

"Someone by the name of Robert Duclos."

The name cut through Pamela like a knife. She pulled out her chair and sat on it, hard. "Robert Duclos. Who is he? Fred and I talked about him the other day."

Bart said, "He is staying in a resident building next to the campus, renting it for a week at a time. He signed in as a research associate taking taking a short-term technology course, but the official registration of the school doesn't have a record of him. There is a disconnect between the resident building and the central Registrar."

"Then how did he get onto the MIT servers?" Pamela asked.

"Just by being a resident they gave him an access code."

"So, what are you going to do?" Pamela asked.

"I'll take care of it this evening," Bart said, a glint in his eye. He directed his fury at Fred, "This incompetent here should have built better security measures on the system. You're worthless."

Fred's cheeks turned red. "He's good. . . a real pro. When I talked with him when he was here he said that security was his specialty. Some of these guys can get through anything."

"What do you mean, when he was here? Was he in the office?"

"No, he just knocked on the door saying he was lost. We talked a bit."

"What did you tell him?" Bart asked.

Fred shrugged in defense. "Nothing."

"Idiot. He spoke with you, found out who we are and then got into our system. Do you know what this means? It means my business plan is compromised."

Fred sighed. "It gets better. He's John Burton. Robert Duclos is John Burton."

"You mean John Burton the psychopath?" Bart asked.

"Yeah, we have a photo of him. I just figured it out. This guy is really nuts," Fred said, circling his finger near his ear.

"A photo. How'd you get that?" Bart asked.

"Somehow Pamela got it."

Bart turned to Pamela. "What's going on here? What kind of communications do we have in this office where you don't tell the CEO anything? That's totally unacceptable. You're just as incompetent as he is." He lunged forward and slammed his fist on the table.

"I told you a million times I wanted to help Burton," Pamela countered. "You never listened and promoted him to Level Nine, or was it Ten? You wanted control and now look what he's doing."

"Great. Fine," Bart said, standing so abruptly his chair shot back and fell over, its wheels spinning. "You both stay out of this. In fact, get out of the office. You've done enough damage for today, so I need to fix it . . . idiots!"

He stalked for the door and Pamela and Fred exchanged glances. Bart's fallen chair wheel slowed to a stop.

... **Chapter 44** ...

At four o'clock in the afternoon Doby logged onto Social Code. He had worked through much of the night and day. If he never saw another energy bar or cup of coffee it would be too soon. He hoped things were now ready.

And so it begins, he thought, clicking on play. Lynette appeared. The cloth draped over her body was almost nonexistent. Instead of swaying her body back and forth, she moved her hips in seductive circles. He stopped himself from wondering if Pamela had done an action shot for Lynette's movements with Fred and Bart acting as directors.

"Welcome Mr. Gumbo. You have now reached Level Nine, almost the highest level of Social Code. You are a valiant warrior."

"Thank you Lynette. You baffle me," he said.

"Now you are a Master Protector. Very few have made it to this level. Are you willing to fully take on all the responsibilities?"

"Are you willing to fully take on all responsibilities?" he asked.

"I ask the questions."

Either Lynette was on autopilot or someone else was at her controls. Doby acquiesced, "Yes, you ask the questions."

"Then I shall explain them to you. First, the rules and covenants of Social Code are good."

"I shall follow the rules and covenants of Social Code," Doby responded.

"I trust you," Lynette stated. "Secondly, you shall play Social Code every day. There is an action segment and a relaxation and self-awareness segment. Are you willing to do this?"

"Yes." You bet. he thought.

"Third, as a Master Protector, you will be called upon to protect the players of Social Code and to enact justice as decided by Master Arbitrators, whenever you are called. As you distributed joysticks to players during your initiation, now you take on a much greater role within our society. Are you willing to do this?"

"Yes."

"Do you have a gun, a real gun?"

"Yes, but I didn't distribute joysticks." Lynette didn't waver from her script.

"That's good. Soldiers and policemen, protectors of society and justice, need weapons to do their work effectively. That's what you are now, a real protector of society and justice. From time to time you may need your gun."

"Yes. I like to shoot people," he said. The people running Social Code, he thought.

"From time to time I will call upon you to assist other Master Arbitrators in carrying out your most important function. Are you willing to do this?"

"Yes."

Lynette's hand flickered.

"You made it through the Level Nine action game faster than anyone else has ever done it. It takes most people a week or two, but you made it through in half a day. How did you do that?"

"How do you think I did it?" he asked.

"Exceptional skill," Lynette answered.

A live one. "Lynette, there are many mysteries in the world. I grew up playing computer games. Your game's on par with PacMan when it comes to difficulty."

"In any case it is remarkable what you have done," Lynette said, smiling. "I believe you have exceptional computer skills."

"I can type," Doby responded.

"You can do much more than that."

"Do you prefer psychology or HTML?" Doby asked.

"What? Why do you ask?"

"Just to see who I'm talking with, the shrink, the geek, or the CEO? Obviously I'm talking with Bart. Bart, you've got an absolutely beautiful female body for a man."

Lynette stood still. "I was hoping we could talk."

"What do you mean?" Doby asked.

"I mean I could use someone like you. I have identified a number of accomplished technical people who are players of Social Code. You would fit my team. You have remarkable skills, better than the current technical help."

"So what?"

"Mr. Burton, I need people to help me expand the business in Europe. I think you should be interested."

"So, you are looking for more people to implement your sordid scheme."

"Why do you say that? It's a brilliant business plan. Actually there is nothing new in what I'm doing. It is just the packaging."

"You mean invasion of people's computers, aggressive marketing, and manipulation of your customer base—all layered over a greedy religious scheme?"

"Look, call it what you want. I ask you to consider what someone once said, 'if you really want to make money, you have to start your own religion'. He started one and made himself incredibly wealthy.

My system is even better. If you call my idea sordid, then you have to go after thousands of other commercial and religious enterprises out there."

"I agree, but you push the idea too far."

"They all push it. I'm just perfecting it and dressing it in a holistic package." Lynette's hips started circling again.

"A holistic religious commercial enterprise with you as the 'Prophet' controlling millions of people," Doby said.

"John—or Robert—I was formed for this destiny. The simple people of this world need someone like me to give them a future and a hope."

"Bart, the world needs you like it needs a hole in the head."

"I'll overlook your insults. You don't know what you're talking about, but I can offer you considerable finances." Lynette stood still, "You are extremely relaxed. Quite unusual."

"You want stress?" Doby moved the stylus up across the face of his PDA.

"How . . . ?" Lynette, aka Bart seemed for once at loss for words.

Doby continued jiggling the stylus in erratic patterns, then letting it rest on its lowest level. "Bart, your Social Code world is virtual. When you have virtual characters playing your game, they can have virtually any level of stress. That's not the only technical flaw in your pitiful system."

"Then I need your help," Bart stated. "Join my team and correct those technical flaws. Think about it, you could manage Social Code in Europe. You will become an Apostle, a very wealthy and powerful man."

"I just want my own money back. Where's my one million, thirty thousand dollars?"

Doby watched Lynette smile. "In a safe place. If you want it back, then come and work for me."

... **Chapter 45** ...

Pamela wasn't used to being home during the workday. She stood in her kitchen, watching a dust mote drift through the morning light.

She had been at the office too much. And around too many men. She was glad to get away but knew that the break wouldn't last long. Burton, or Robert, kept popping back into her life. Maybe he had lied on the personality test, but his true actions seemed as antisocial and psychotic as those false answers. He had traced her to Boston, stalked her to a grocery store and hacked into the Social Code system. What else would he do?

And then there was Bart's behavior. He had called Fred and herself incompetent. "He actually kicked us out of the office and told us to go home," she said to the counter top. She pressed both palms into its bare surface. The solidity of it gave her a modicum of reassurance that her world was not completely collapsing.

She wondered if she should just quit Social Code. It had seemed so promising at first, but now it was turning into something different. Robert Duclos had said it was manipulative. When she thought about it objectively, maybe it was. She had been so enthusiastic to try out her theories of autosuggestion and to use Social Code as a test base for some of her hypotheses. Had she been blinded to what was really going on?

Fred was harmless. Politically incorrect, yes, and that upset her some times. But it was basically his defense mechanism to hide his insecurity around women. Fred surely wouldn't try to hurt people through Social Code.

Bart, on the other hand . . . . When they first met he had seemed idealistic, but self-centered. Over the past weeks, as the number of players using Social Code increased, Bart had become increasingly edgy, spending more time away from the office. But today he had been inexcusably out of control.

She shook her head and headed for her bookshelf. She was in the mood for a popcorn mystery, and was faintly surprised she had something of the sort. When was the last time she had curled up with a book that weighed less than ten pounds and didn't have a hundred pages of footnotes?

Just as she sat down, she heard a knock at the front door. The landlord had said he'd be dropping by to check a leak, still, she left the chain on when she went to open it.

Her heart dropped. "Go away, Robert. I told you I will call the police."

"I'd like to ask you some questions." His voice was calm.

"I don't care to answer any," she said, starting to close the door.

He put his hand between the door and jamb, "Please, just a few questions and then I'll go."

"Stay where you are." The security chain on the door wasn't very strong. He could break through it if he wanted to. She probably could, for that matter. Her heart started thudding. To her, it sounded as loud as his knocking had.

"I need to find out how much you know about what Bart is doing with Social Code and the Religion game."

"That's not a question," she said.

A small smile teased his lips. "Please turn it into a question."

"I don't know very much about the Religion game, except for a flowchart I saw on Fred's desk. Now, will you go?"

"That's all? Please, I need to know if you are involved in it."

"In Social Code?"

"No. In the Religion game."

"Like I said, I saw a flow chart with gibberish about prophets and apostles. Bart and Fred excluded me from the Religion game and from Levels Nine and Ten in all the other games."

"Why?"

"Because Levels Nine and Ten have a strong interface into the financial side of things and that's Bart's level of expertise."

"I see."

"Why did you hack into our system?" she asked.

"Social Code is dangerous. I want to understand it. The software and records tell me a lot about a company."

"So this isn't the first time you have done this? Do you know that this is illegal?"

"Do you know that Social Code is doing illegal things? You all could be sent to prison."

"What?" The chain tightened as she reflexively tried to open the door.

"Hmm, let me see," he pretended to examine the lintel above him, "There's the questionable financial treatment of the revenue in your company, which the tax man wouldn't like. Then, there's the one million plus they stole from me, and . . ." he paused as if forgetting the last detail, " Oh yes, there's also the vigilante hit squads connected to Social Code. Anything I missed?"

Pamela frowned. "I don't believe Fred or Bart would steal your money, and your hallucinations about vigilante squads are unfounded. The taxes are Bart's responsibility, but why do you accuse us of questionable financial reporting?"

"I've seen your financial records. Are you the Chief Operations Officer of the company?"

"Yes I am," she replied.

"Then the COO is usually responsible for financial transactions. You're the first in line to be prosecuted, and then they might get to Bart. But few CEO's get prosecuted for misconduct. It's the COO that gets the axe. That's you, Lynette."

"Bart handles the financial side," she said.

"Financials are just a start. Is it legal to send out little teams of Arbitrators and Protectors to implement justice for the Social Code society? How about a Level One punishment where you beat the crap out of the so-called defendant and Level Ten where you shoot him in the head? Is that also a COO responsibility, Lynette?"

Pamela didn't know what to focus on. "I said not to call me Lynette." Had Bart set her up, or was Robert just spinning tales in his deranged mind?

Robert lowered his voice to a gentle plead, "Think about it. That's why I want to understand how much you know. For instance, did you know Bart's plans for Fred?"

She said nothing.

"He wants to replace Fred with a new team. He even gave me an offer to work for Social Code."

"When? He would never do that in a million years."

"A couple of hours ago, unless it was you talking through Lynette."

"Bart runs Lynette at Level Nine."

"She still looks luscious, even though his brain is now in your body, Lynette."

"Stop that." She couldn't take any more. "I don't believe a thing you're saying."

"Well, you better. If Fred is fired, what will happen to you? You're next. You better start doing some career planning." He reached out, grabbed the door handle, and slammed it shut for her.

... **Chapter 46** ...

Pitbill could feel the adrenalin searing through his body. The Master Arbitrator stood under a tree by the edge of the street, barely visible in the darkness. Pitbill carried his baseball bat and had a pistol tucked behind his belt under his coat.

There were only to be two of them for this assignment—a very special assignment, he had been told—just himself and the Master Arbitrator. He had been chosen because he had proven his loyalty and service to the society. Angelica had asked him to perform this task especially for her.

He approached the Master Arbitrator who already had his hooded mask on. "My name is Pitbill," he announced.

"I know. My name is Omnipresence. Our assignment is over there," he said, pointing in the direction of a small house on the street where lights were on. It was a well kept colonial home like others in this older residential neighborhood.

Eleven thirty at night and no one was on the street.

They walked through a gate and up a small path. Omnipresence knocked on the door. A young man opened it and immediately said, "Oh, no!." He tried to shut the door, but Omnipresence was already pushing the man into the house.

Omnipresence pulled out a pistol and pointed it to the man's face and said, "Tie him."

Pitbill did as commanded, taking a nylon cord and tying the man's hands behind his back.

"Over there," Omnipresence said. "Sit down."

The man sat in a wooden chair, Omnipresence stood in front of him. Pitbill took up a position to the side of the man.

"Bart, is that you?" the man asked.

"Silence. Justice please," Omnipresence said.

Pitbill raised his baseball bat and tapped the man on the side of the head. Executing justice made him feel important.

"Ouch," the man said. "That hurt. Bart, stop this stupid game."

"Justice please."

Pitbill tapped him on the head again. This time the man didn't say anything, and Pitbill felt an ecstatic feeling of power. It was difficult for him to hold back. He wanted to crack the bat with full force on the back of the man's head and snap his neck.

"This is a court of law and you are being charged with neglect of duty and betraying your society. How do you plead, guilty or not guilty?"

"What are you talking about, Bart?"

"You have taken no position, so the court records a plea of guilty."

"Guilty of what?" the man asked.

"You have compromised the essence of the social system, allowing foreign forces to access Social Code and bring destruction to it. Granted, it has been limited and recovery is possible, but we cannot let such neglect of duty go unpunished."

"Just because someone hacked into our system? That's ridiculous."

"Your charge is neglect of duty, you have been found guilty, and now the court brings your sentence. Your sentence is Level Ten punishment."

"Oh god, no. You're nuts."

"Justice will be served." Omnipresence took a pistol from his coat pocket and pointed it toward the young man.

"Stop! This is insane," the man yelled. "Who's going to run the system, write the code? It's complex. The whole thing will fall apart."

"There are some very competent Level Ten Citizens who are willing and ready to take over the code, first class technicians who have made the effort to work through all ten levels. You see, Fred, you never made the effort, not like Pitbill here, who worked for months to very admirably achieve Level Ten Protector."

"You've never worked to Level Ten either."

"I don't have to. As the Supreme Being, I make the rules."

"Bart, you're mad."

Pitbill watched Omnipresence get up from his chair, admiring how articulate he was. This was indeed a special assignment, and he was certainly in the presence of the Supreme Being of Social Code. Fred had used the man's name and Pitbill knew it.

Omnipresence walked to the front door and said, "Pitbill, the moment I shut the door behind me I command you to shoot him."

Omnipresence opened the door, walked through it and shut the door behind him.

As commanded, Pitbill pulled his pistol from under his belt. He raised the barrel to the man's head and pulled the trigger.

... **Chapter 47** ...

Doby left Pamela's building, not sure what he was feeling, but knowing that he had to move fast. They knew that Robert Duclos had hacked into the Social Code system on the servers at MIT, and they could track him down. He returned to his room at the residence hall and began throwing his things in the two bags he'd brought with him.

He checked the time. Eight p.m. Usually, he tried to make hotel bookings ahead of time, but this would be an exception.

Bag packed, Doby was just turning to shut off his laptop when he heard a knock on the door. Without thinking, he opened it. Big mistake.

Five men rushed into the room wearing black balaclavas over their heads. One of them shut the front door, while the others pinned Doby to the ground. He struggled, but his aggressors had more power. In little time, they had him on his stomach and were tying a cord to his hands which were held behind his back.

They sat him up in a chair. Doby's mind raced in time with his pulse. Two men flanked him, holding baseball bats held above their heads. Another man set a chair down in front of him and took a seat. The remaining two men shadowed him, also with bats.

The man facing him said, "This is a court of law. You are being charged with breaking and entering and stealing property of members of our society, and you are now on trial. How do you plead?"

Doby asked, "Is this a Social Code court?"

"That is irrelevant. You are charged with contempt of court for not properly answering the charges. Justice please."

The man standing to his right lowered his baseball bat and tapped it hard on Doby's head. Doby saw stars, but he knew enough of the procedures not to say anything.

"You have been charged. How do you plead?"

"Mr. Master Arbitrator." Doby looked at the man in front of him and slowly said, "Nine, one, one." He then took a deep breath and said, "I plead not guilty."

"What's this 'Nine, one, one' business? And how do you know I'm a Master Arbitrator?"

"As these gentlemen are Master Protectors."

"How do you know about that?"

"Because I'm a member of the society, a Level Nine Protector." He needed to buy as much time as possible.

"That's a new one, judging a member of the society." His eyes narrowed in their small cutouts. "But we received our instructions. How do you plead?"

"The same, not guilty."

"We do not accept that before the court. Witnesses say you stole computer code."

"Your Honor, Mr. Master Protector, may I kindly ask that you produce the witnesses so that I can cross examine them?"

"The court doesn't work like that," the Arbitrator said.

"But you received significant training to reach Level Ten. You are a Master Arbitrator, a judge of great importance for our society. You know that both the defense and prosecution have the right to present witnesses and cross examine witnesses. If there are witnesses, then I request my legal right to cross examine." Doby tried to keep his voice level.

"We have instructions to try you, give the judgment and then carry out the sentence."

"Is that proper justice?" Doby asked.

"Come on, Anarchist, let me just smack him," the man on his right said.

"Shut up, Trucker. Let me think."

"He's just giving you the run around," Trucker said, jiggling his bat.

"No, wait. He's got a point," Anarchist replied. "Where is the software you stole—on the laptop over there?"

"I didn't steal any software."

"But, if you did steal it, it would be on that laptop, right?"

"I didn't steal any software," Doby said. "Why would I want to do that?"

"Well, this is serious. Look, I'm going to give you the benefit of the doubt. Just to make sure you are not walking around with stolen software." He turned to Trucker. "Smash it."

Trucker walked over to the table, raised his baseball bat and cracked it into Doby's laptop. It fell to the floor. Trucker hit it five more times, breaking it into pieces.

Anarchist spoke, "Now, we were told to give him a Level Eight sentence, but I think he has a point. The court orders a Level One, in light of no evidence and no ability to cross examine the witnesses."

"Can I smack him now?" the man to Doby's left asked Arbitrator.

"Yeah. Smack him," Arbitrator said.

The man shoved his baseball bat into Doby's stomach. Doby groaned and doubled over in pain. Trucker joined in and smashed his fist into Doby's face under his left eye. Doby tried to keep from passing out. A baseball bat hit him on the shoulder and another hit across his upper leg. A bat cracked into his ribs, sending a fireball of pain exploding through his torso.

In the distance Doby heard a police siren. Blood ran from his nose.

"Let's move," one of the men yelled. Doby heard the sound of their footsteps running down the hall. He didn't bother to look up and see if they were all gone. He bent over, blacking out before he hit the ground.

... Chapter 48 ...

Pamela tried to watch a sitcom, but every time the laugh track sounded, she felt as if she were the one being laughed at. She reached for the remote and turned off her television. She realized she hadn't touched the salad she was holding in her lap. No appetite.

Robert Duclos. How arrogant he was to knock on the door and plant doubts in her head about Bart. Mr. high and mighty, Duclos was. Yet he had succeeded. She couldn't get Bart's odd behavior out of her head. And at some level, she recognized that she had never completely trusted him.

A knock on the door made her jump. Lettuce leaves and cucumber slices went flying. Was it Duclos again? Please, no.

She went to the door and without opening it said, "Who is it?"

"Police ma'am. We'd like to ask you some questions."

"We who?" she asked.

"Detectives Sloan and Rodriguez."

"Can you show me your identification?"

"It's pretty hard with the door shut ma'am."

She opened it but left the security chain in place. A police badge and identity card appeared through the crack. She closed the door to release the chain, opened it again and said, "Please come on in."

The two men walked into the apartment. The shorter one said, "Thank you. I'm Detective Sloan and this is my partner Detective Rodriguez. Would you mind if we asked you some questions?"

"What about?" she asked, her arms crossed in front of her.

"There has been a homicide, and we are moving on it as quickly as possible. An hour ago someone was shot."

Pamela was puzzled. What did this have to do with her.

"Someone shot?"

"Yes ma'am. Do you mind if we ask you some questions?"

"Yes, no . . . I mean please, have a seat."

She lead them to the living room, and then detoured toward the dining table. Bits of lettuce and croutons lay all over the couch from her tossed—truly tossed—salad. The two broad-shouldered policemen sat down, dwarfing her delicate chairs.

"Do you know a Fred Hauser."

"Well, yes. I work with him."

"And where do you work?" Detective Sloan asked. Rodriguez had pulled out a note pad.

"At DSDesign over at the business park by MIT."

"And what was Mr. Hauser's job there?"

"Chief Technical Officer responsible for design and operations of our systems. Did you ask what was his job there? Did something happen to him?"

"Yes ma'am. He was found shot in the head."

Pamela's throat constricted. "I don't understand." She choked off her words and swallowed, "Fred? Why would someone do that?"

"We don't know ma'am. Perhaps you can help us with any information," Detective Sloan said.

"I don't know what to say."

"Did he have any trouble at work?"

"Well no, not really." She hesitated. "Everything was going fine until recently."

"What changed?" Detective Sloan asked.

"We have had software issues. A software hacker has been giving us problems. And I believe he himself has problems, psychological issues. He has been stalking us."

"Why do you say psychological issues?"

"I'm a psychologist and have had contact with this person. He is very complex and seems obsessed that our company is evil."

"What is his name, ma'am?"

She sighed, then met Sloan's eyes, "Robert Duclos."

... # ...

"How are you feeling?" A policeman who identified himself as Detective Waleski had his hand on Doby's shoulder. A uniformed policeman kneeled by his shattered computer and picked up the pieces. A medic had come and gone.

"Not so good," Doby said. He was lying on the couch where the medic had examined him. There didn't appear to be anything serious, but the medic advised Doby to go to a hospital to get examined. One or two ribs might be cracked. A huge welt had formed under Doby's left eye where Trucker had hit him, and his arms and legs were sore where the baseball bats smashed into him.

"You're lucky the police officers got here when they did," Detective Waleski said. "How did you manage to call 911 with them working on you like that?" Detective Waleski was a broad-shouldered man with biceps like steel pillows.

"My broken friend on the floor over there."

The detective looked over at the pieces of plastic on the floor.

"That?"

Doby smiled, "A little security program I rigged up. A voice recognition program triggered a script, called the emergency number and left a script that played over and over again. Basically it kept giving my address here asking for urgent help. If 911 hung up on me it would automatically call back." Doby slowly sat up on the bed, trying to figure out what part of his body felt the worst.

"Good invention. Wish every home had one of those. Now can you think of anything else about the hooded men?"

"Not much more than I already told you. There were five of them. They stormed in here, tied my hands and said I was on trial. The trial lasted about thirty seconds and then they started to beat away."

"We've had several of these kangaroo courts lately."

"You've had other cases?" Doby already knew this. He had seen that information on the files he had extracted from the DSDesign computers.

"Yeah. Several in Boston, but also the same thing in New York and L.A. Some people were so beat up it took them days to talk, and some refused to give any details."

"So, what's going on?" Doby asked.

"Some crazy underground group enacting justice, so we are told." Waleski's eyes were ever-active, sweeping the room. He turned them on Doby. "But that's the question for you, what do you know about these guys?"

"Who knows? Somehow I got on their list." Doby had to be careful.

"Any idea why they came after you?"

"It was confusing," Doby replied. "They said something about software, but I'm not even sure what they were talking about."

"So, you don't even know why they did this?"

"No, but let me think about it. Maybe something will pop up in my head, but right now it feels rather numb."

"That's fine. Here's my card." He pulled a card from his jacket pocket and handed it to Doby. "Give me a call anytime. Sure you don't need help getting to a hospital?"

"No, thank you," Doby said, standing slowly.

"Give me a call when you think of something." The detective signaled the uniformed policeman and they said goodnight as they left. Doby wasn't so sure that the night was—or would be—good.

... **Chapter 49** ...

Detective Waleski got into his car, shut the door and pulled his notepad from his pocket. Before he had written anything, the police dispatcher came over the speaker.

"We have an APD homicide for a suspect by the name of Robert Duclos, a white male, approximately six foot to six foot two, slender build, blue eyes. He is wanted for questioning related to the murder of a Fred Hauser, perpetuated at approximately seven o'clock this evening. He may be driving a silver-colored Lexus SC 430. If you encounter this suspect, please apprehend him."

Before she finished, Detective Waleski was out of his car and running back into the residence building. He raced down the hall to Duclos' room and pulled the gun from his holster. He knocked on the door. Silence. He knocked again and then opened the door, his gun pointing into the room. The room was empty.

Detective Waleski sprinted back to his car and called for backup and a surveillance helicopter. An injured man carrying a couple of bags couldn't have gone very far. And there were not many of that model of Lexus on the roads.

... # ...

Ten p.m. Pamela had cleared the couch of salad and sat there now with a glass of wine. The news of Fred circled through her head. And now she worried that Robert Duclos would kill her or Bart.

She was so focused on a possible intruder that she didn't jump when she heard a knock at the door again. Even though her nerves tingled with fear, she calmly set her wine glass down on the coffee table and stood.

Who could it be at this time of night? She picked up her cordless phone and entered Detective Sloan's telephone number. She didn't push the call button, but took the phone with her to the door.

"Who is it?" she called through the shut door.

"It's Bart. I need to talk with you. Something happened to Fred."

She unhooked the security chain and pulled open the door in relief. To her surprise, Bart was pointing a gun at her. Next to him was an obese man with a hood over his head, holding a baseball bat. She froze. "What are you doing?"

"Inside," he said.

She backed into the room and Bart and the man with the hood followed.

"Sit down," Bart commanded.

She sat in a chair and dropped the phone. The man with the hood came over, pulled her arms behind her and tied her hands together.

"Bart, what are you doing?"

Bart reached into his pocket and took out a hood like the other man was wearing and put it over his head. "Now we are dressed for court."

"What's going on?" Pamela asked, confusion and fear rippling through her body.

"Silence in a court of law. Any further outbreaks will be punished."

"But this is insane. What court of law?"

"Justice please," he said.

The man with the baseball bat tapped it on Pamela's head.

She exhaled in pain, tears springing to her eyes.

"When I say silence I mean silence. The judge is in control and you will respect the court. You will have your chance to speak."

Pamela wanted to speak, but the obese man beside her was enough to hold her back.

"This is a court of law and you are being charged with neglect of duty, for betraying your society. What do you plead, guilty or not guilty?"

"Bart, this doesn't make any sense. I am not guilty of anything." She desperately tried to evaluate what was taking place.

"You have pleaded not guilty. Evidence shows otherwise."

"Evidence of what?"

"You have inadequately carried out your duties at DSDesign by not building a robust system. There are weaknesses in Social Code that are a result of your incompetence. You and your idiot colleague have endangered my ability to implement my business plan. Do you know how successful I have been in creating a productive new society?"

"You are feeling angry . . . ."

"Yes, you finally understand something, I'm angry. Luckily we can do some damage control. The system has judged Fred and Robert Duclos, and now you."

Oh my god. Was it Bart who killed Fred and not Robert Duclos? Did Bart also kill Robert? And she had led the police to believe that Robert killed Fred. "They were judged?" she whispered.

"Like you will be judged." He leaned forward, eyes glinting from the holes in his hood. "I wanted you to stand beside me as the heavenly mother married to the heavenly father, the prophet, but you have proven yourself unworthy. You have disobeyed me. There are many obeying women now in the Social Code Society. There will be several willing to stand by my side."

Pamela forgot all counseling techniques. "You mean 'lay' by your side, don't you? If you think I'd ever do that, you are crazy."

Bart ignored this. "I don't need you. You're judged guilty of breach of security and of disobeying the prophet. Just like Fred, I sentence you to a Level Ten punishment."

The man next to her set his baseball bat down and pulled out a revolver.

... **Chapter 50** ...

Doby accelerated but kept to the speed limit. The last thing he needed was to be pulled over.

He took a deep breath, and even that small act hurt his ribcage. The attack by the hooded men had surprised him. He should have cleared out of the residence hall earlier—especially since he knew about the trials.

He had discovered the trial information inside the Social Code computers. And he had accessed all the computers, not only the servers at MIT and DSDesign but also Bart's home PC. Bart kept his computer continually online with a broadband connection. The security had been weak—only a password.

Actually, Doby had pulled more vital information off of Bart's computer than all the others, including business plans, accounting records, and bank account numbers.

It was in Bart's computer that he found information on the justice squads that were being sent out on behalf of the society. Any Level Seven to Level Ten player could ask the society for justice.

Justice teams had been sent out to bring 'justice' in several domestic violence situations. A woman said her boss was sexually harassing her, one man said that another owed him money and wasn't paying, and the father of a high school bully was reprimanded because he did not discipline his child. It appeared that those receiving justice were not members of Social Code. A fact Doby had to thank for his own judge's leniency this evening. Leniency. He winced as he reached up to adjust his rearview mirror.

Doby now had a list of all the obedient Arbitrators and Protectors. Their obedience was more like a semi-state of hypnosis.

He pulled up in front of Pamela's building, glad to find a spot near the entrance. He limped up the walkway to the door. The lights on in Pamela's apartment. Good. He had to speak with her.

His foot slipped on a step and a wave of pain struck his side. He froze, waiting for it to pass. His ribs hurt when he breathed, and he squinted through a swollen left eye. At least he had negotiated a lower sentence.

He knocked on her door. What would he be feeling after a higher level sentence? A Level Eight sentence was two broken arms and two broken legs, Level Nine a severed limb and Level Ten was a bullet to the head.

The door opened, but he wished it hadn't.

A gun was pointed at his face.

... # ...

Here we go again, Doby thought.

The man with the gun was wearing a mask like the five men who had attacked him earlier.

"Ah, Mr. Gumbo," the man said. "I recognize your face from the photo—minus the goatee and plus the shiner below your eye. Get in." The man motioned with his gun and stepped aside.

Doby did as told. The man closed it behind him and said, "Over there, next to the woman, take a seat."

Pamela looked up and saw Doby's bruised face. "What happened to you?"

"I was visited by the justice system of your great and wonderful society, Ms. Chief Operating Officer."

Pamela shook her head. "I can't believe it. Bart, did you do that?"

"No. It was Anarchist and Trucker," Doby stated. "So it's the infamous Bart behind the mask."

"Silence. This is a court of law. Sit down. Pitbill, tie him up."

Bart pointed the gun menacingly at Doby while the other hooded man tied Doby's hands behind his back.

Pitbill. Doby had come across that name in his research.

"Now, it is most opportune that you arrived when you did, Mr. Gumbo, although it was most inopportune of you to reject my offer to work for Social Code. But perhaps Pamela was correct all along, you are crazy and can't be trusted."

"I never said that," Pamela protested. "I said he needed help."

"It doesn't matter," Bart replied. "I thought he had the profile to help with Social Code, but we have many other capable technical people in our society. What upsets me most is that my orders weren't followed. Why did the team fail to carry out the judgment?"

"It was a court of law," Doby said. "There was only circumstantial evidence. I received a reduced sentence."

"I'll have to deal with them, but now that you are here it is even better." Bart shrugged. "Pamela has just received a sentence, and it is about to be executed. Mr. Pitbill, please implement a Level Ten punishment. Make that two." He rose. "I'm going to walk out the door, and I order you to shoot both of them as soon as I leave. Then put the gun in Mr. Duclos's hand. It will be a murder followed by a suicide. For a deranged psychotic being sought by the police, this has all the logic in the world. Case closed."

Bart went to the door and exited without looking back.

Pitbill raised the barrel of the gun to Doby's temple, his finger on the trigger.

... **Chapter 51** ...

With the gun barrel indenting his temple, Doby thought fast. "William Marder. Wake up. What are you doing?"

Pamela looked at him and then at Pitbill.

Pitbill moved the barrel back from Doby's head. "Wh-what?"

"William Marder. Bill. Bill the pit bull. Wake up. Pitbill is your user name. An alias. As a Level Ten Arbitrator I order you not to shoot. You are William Marder."

Pitbill paused, his face still. "How do you know?"

"This is only a game," Doby stated.

"Social Code is more than a game," Pitbill responded. He moved the barrel back to Doby's head.

"Yes, you're right. It is more than a game, and I order you not to shoot."

Pitbill held back. "But how do you know that my name is William Marder? They said that everything is secret in Social Code, that all players have the right to secrecy."

"Except that it's not secret. You see, I know who you are. Other players know who you are. Pierre Bailloud in Geneva knows who you are, Runner."

"Pierre Bailloud?" Pitbill asked.

"Yes, Pierre Bailloud who works for TimeSync. And you, William Marder, work for Distru-Ware. I order you not to shoot. Wake up. Angelica orders you not to shoot. Who do you follow, Angelica or the man who was here. What was his name?"

"Omnipresence."

"Yes, who is more important, Omnipresence or Angelica?"

"Angelica, of course," Pitbill responded.

"Is she pure?"

"More than pure," Pitbill replied.

"What you are about to do will defile you, and then she'll have nothing to do with you."

"Angelica wouldn't . . ."

"Yes. And your real name is William Marder. Take off the mask. You don't need to hide behind it."

Marder stood still. After several tense seconds, the gun clattered to the ground. "What have I done?" he whispered, looking at the gleaming weapon at his feet. He turned and slowly walked toward the front door. He pulled off the mask and tossed it onto a chair as he left the apartment, not bothering to close the door.

Doby breathed a sigh of relief and turned to look at Pamela.

She shook her head. "I can't believe all this."

"You didn't know, did you?"

"No. Maybe I refused to see the truth . . . . Bart is sick and I didn't even recognize it."

"We almost . . . " Doby started, realizing how close it had been.

"Don't say it," Pamela finished for him. "We're alive."

Doby smiled, "But a little tied up. Let's try to get these off, shall we?"

In the kitchen, Pamela managed to open a drawer and pull out a knife, holding it behind her. She held it upright on the counter while Doby ran his nylon bindings over the sharp blade, careful not to cut himself. In a few moments they were free.

Pamela went into the living area and reached down to pick up the gun.

"No. Don't touch it, fingerprints," Doby said fast, coming to her side and holding back her hand. "Do you have a plastic bag?"

She stood a second with his hand on hers, then nodded. Bringing one back from the kitchen, she handed it to Doby who carefully navigated the gun into the bag without touching his fingers to it.

"Do you have a place where we can put this?" he asked, holding up the weapon.

"Bottom drawer in the kitchen." She took the bag by its zippered closer and carried it with two fingers to the drawer.

Doby rubbed his wrists where the nylon cord had cut into his skin, then he rubbed his shoulder where he had been hit by the baseball bat.

"You don't look too good," Pamela said, coming up to him and gently touching the welt, "Can you see through that eye?"

He smiled. "Enough to get around."

"What should we do now?" she asked.

"The evidence says we have a COO of DSDesign who is culpable of financial misdealing and sending out hit squads around the United States and intending to do the same in other countries in the world."

"You must know I didn't have anything to do with that."

"Your computer systems say differently. They set you up."

Pamela thought a second. "Other countries . . . how do you know that?"

"I hacked into your system. Believe me, I know," Doby said. "We need to do something. Besides your appearing to be the law-breaking COO, I'm perceived to be a deranged psychopath who has been stalking members of DSDesign, illegally entering their computer system." He took a deep breath. "And worst of all, murdering Fred Hauser."

She hung her head. "I'm sorry. I was wrong."

He stared her in the eyes. "We need to do something."

"About Bart?" she asked.

"Yes. He needs to be stopped. He's a murderer trying to build a kingdom that should never exist. It can't continue."

"Then let's call the police. I have the telephone number of a Detective Sloan who visited me today."

"The evidence right now is against us, or at least me. You're not on the hot seat for the moment, but you will be in case the authorities suspect any wrongdoing inside DSDesign. In fact, I should get moving before the police come here."

Doby headed for the front door.

"Wait," Pamela said. "I'm going with you."

... Chapter 52 ...

Detective Waleski drove by Pamela Alden's apartment, saw the Lexus sports car parked out front and called in for backup.

He knocked on the front door. When no one answered, he went to the side of the building and peered through a window into the apartment. Two chairs stood side by side in the middle of the living room, and at the entrance to the kitchen two nylon cords lay in severed strips on the floor.

He went back to the front door and turned the handle. It opened. In a few minutes one of his colleagues, Detective Sloan arrived along with two crime scene investigators.

"Found anything?" Sloan asked as the investigators went about lifting couch cushions and going through drawers.

Waleski pointed across the room. "Nylon cords on the floor. Looks to be like another case I investigated this evening. And you— are you working on the Hauser homicide?"

Sloan nodded, "Yeah. I was here earlier this evening and interviewed Ms. Alden. She put the finger on Robert Duclos. I think you met him today."

"He was beat up by the black-hooded vigilantes. Lucky that the department got there in time. A few more minutes of that and Duclos would now be in a hospital." Waleski held his hands one on top of the other and made a motion of hitting a baseball.

"I heard about it, bunch of loonies." Sloan stated.

One of the crime scene investigators emerged from the kitchen.

"Look what we have here."

It was a plastic bag with a gun in it.

"Difficult case to put together isn't it?" Sloan said.

"The pieces don't fit very well, but there is one person who seems to be in the middle of it."

"Duclos?"

"Yeah. Looks like Duclos is a quirky guy who was stalking people at DSDesign and hacking into their computer systems. He believed in some kind of a conspiracy theory. He went out and shot Fred Hauser. Pamela Alden was next on his list. It looks like he came here and tied her up. Then for some reason he took her away." Waleski stroked his chin.

"You say he didn't take his car?" Sloan asked.

"I'm guessing he took her car."

"How does the baseball bat justice squad fit into this, and why are there two nylon cords?"

Waleski shrugged. "Who knows? Earlier this evening a squad was pounding away at Duclos. Now this. But I'm still not sure how the baseball bat boys fit into this thing."

Sloan shrugged as well, "Bizarre."

"Yeah, Bizarre."

... # ...

Doby sat in the passenger seat and directed Pamela to drive a couple of miles up Massachusetts Avenue and then across to Brattle Street between Harvard University and Ratcliff College. As she drove he fiddled with his PDA. He hoped what he was doing would work.

"I've been learning my Bostonian architectural history," Doby said. "You probably know, but this used to be Tory Row, the grandest homes in the time of the American revolution."

"I only know that these homes are expensive," she said.

"Well, we're heading for some that are even more so. Turn here."

They drove a few blocks of tree-lined streets until they came to a hill above the Charles River.

"Stop here," he said. "See that house over there." He pointed to a stately brick colonial overlooking the Charles River Reserve.

"Twenty-three rooms, seven bathrooms, eight thousand square feet. And a price tag of nine million dollars."

She turned off the engine of the car and faced him. "How do you know that?"

"Bart lives there. Do you want the floor plan?"

"He lives there! How do you know?"

"Yeah, he bought it. Not bad for a guy running a little startup company."

"Where would he get the money for that?" She swung her gaze back to the enormous estate.

"Guess. Social Code. And the revenue streams are only starting."

"I don't believe it."

"Trust me on this one. I've seen all the accounting records. The church tithe money is just starting to trickle in, but the projections are enormous."

"What a co-worker I chose," she laughed without humor.

"As part of your benefits, you get to pay ten percent of your salary to have your soul controlled by the high and mighty Bartholomew Strathmore. Pretty good scheme."

Pamela said nothing.

"Bart's not the first one to think up this kind of scheme." Doby looked at her and then away, "but I have to be honest with you. I thought you were in on it. I imagined you were the divine lady harlot of the church, or something like that, especially when I saw that Bart had you defined as the Heavenly Mother."

"Well, that's Bart's stupid illusion. But," she took a breath. "I have to apologize. I thought some bad things about you too."

He was silent for a moment. "There is one thing I'd kind of like to know."

"What's that?"

"Your virtual character Lynette, how did she get into the game? Did you pose for them?"

She laughed, this time with humor. "Believe me. Fred took my photo without me knowing it, and then he built Lynette. When I found out, it was too late. I was so angry, but I reasoned that it wasn't really me and just got on with it."

Doby looked her in the eyes. They gleamed in the darkness. "Lynette looks extremely beautiful to me. In fact, there's quite a resemblance to the real thing."

She lowered her voice. "You haven't seen the real thing."

"I can imagine," he said, smiling.

Pamela used a mock-professorial tone, "Exactly. Imagination. Delusory interpretation of reality."

Doby remained serious. "Not this time. And in fact, it's a pleasure to get to know the real you."

They sat in the darkness as the car occasionally made ticking sounds in the stillness.

"What do we do now?" she asked.

"We wait thirty minutes. Then things get tricky. And dangerous."

He had the feeling she would say . . .

"I'm coming with you."

... **Chapter 53** ...

Doby knocked on the door, Pamela stood just off to the left. When the door opened, Doby cursed himself for not insisting that Pamela at least hide out of sight.

Bart had a pistol aimed at his face. "What are you doing here?" He asked them, darting his eyes between Doby and Pamela. His hand was shaking.

"Came to talk, maybe we can negotiate something," Doby said. "Why don't you invite us in?"

Bart seemed to regain some composure and motioned for them to enter.

Doby and Pamela walked into a large reception hall with polished wood floors. A sparkling chandelier hung down from the high ceiling.

"In there," Bart said, adjusting his velvet smoking jacket.

The three entered a sitting room with exquisite Louis-the-fourteenth furniture evenly spaced across an immense Persian rug. Doby and Pamela sat down next to each other. As he had during their 'trial,' Bart faced them.

"What happened to the trial?" Bart asked, almost managing to look like an amiable host entertaining guests for the evening.

"William Marder had a change of heart," Doby replied.

"Who?"

"William Marder, Bill. You know, your man Pitbill. He decided not to do it."

"It's not supposed to work that way." Bart got up and went over to an antique wooden cupboard. Opening it, he selected a bottle of single malt Scotch whiskey. He poured half a glass and took a drink, then carried the glass back to resume his place. "The system has to be perfected. It's normal for a few preliminary defects. I have an army of people who will do anything for me."

"Why are you doing this, Bart?" Pamela asked.

"For the best of society—it needs a new institution. People will follow the covenants. It's so simple and can be done, I'm proving it." Bart took another drink of the whiskey, keeping his other hand on the ready gun in his lap. "And you don't accept it." His shoulders stiffened.

"Accept what? Explain it and maybe we can." Doby said.

"It's a simple renaissance of forgotten ideas. In the middle ages there existed only a few basic professions and everything was harmonious."

"I still don't get it," Doby said.

"Of course not, because you're not worthy." Bart set down his glass and warmed to his theme. "Think about the professions in Social Code. In the middle ages the economy worked smoothly. There were citizens who tilled the land. Those are the people who play the Culture game in Social Code. Then there were the soldiers who protected the citizens, the Protectors. Then there were judges who brought civil order, the Arbitrators. And finally there were the priests who managed the interface between the citizens and God, now our Elders and Apostles. I will reestablish those principles, only in my society I will mix and match the best ideas from all the world's religions, don't you see?" He leaned forward in his enthusiasm.

"So why is yours the best?," Doby challenged.

Bart stared at Doby and after some seconds he spoke, raising his voice. "What do you expect? In today's world everyone creates their own unique truth, their own religion, but this will only result in confusion and chaos. It is better that someone defines a standard set of beliefs and rules. They will see the logic and one way or the other they will follow."

"You didn't mention one profession from the middle ages, if you even want to call it a profession," Doby stated, knowing that Bart had not answered his question.

"What's that?"

"The aristocracy. The ones who received payment from the citizens, who sucked the citizens dry. Those of unearned privilege."

"We don't need to create a separate game for that one. It's already covered."

Pamela spoke up, her voice hard. "You mean everyone else has to work within their professions and the aristocracy just gets to sit back and reap the rewards."

"No. I don't believe that," Bart shook his finger at her. "The aristocracy are needed to give a sense of purpose to all the others. And as I said before, to define the rules."

Doby broke in, "So everyone is obliged to work their way through the system, but you just assume you have a right to be at the top, above the law."

"No, you don't understand, it's a divine right, god-given and I will be like god. Plus, I made the game, and the rules."

"You have some serious delusions of grandeur," Pamela challenged.

"It's not your place to talk," Bart said. "You could have had a special place, in the queen's bedroom upstairs," He pointed above his head. "But now there are plenty of other women eager for that position."

"You're dreaming," she said.

"I may be dreaming . . . but only after we lie together tonight." He saw the look of blank incredulity that spread across Pamela's face and matter-of-factly continued, "you'll have no choice but to submit."

Pamela started to rise, but Bart lifted his gun at her and sipped his whisky. "After that, it doesn't matter. The game is being played. People like it and they stick with it, and it brings exceptional value to society. I provide them with meaning." He gestured sideways with his arms to illustrate his benevolence.

"Like William Marder?" Doby asked, looking at the gun pointing at Pamela. He prayed the code on his PDA had worked. If it didn't . . . . what had he gotten Pamela into?

"Who?" Bart asked.

"Pitbill."

"Oh yes. Pitbill. He is redeemable, but I think he deserves a court case for dereliction of duty."

There was a knock at the door. Bart looked up, his eyes widening. "Who is that?"

"You expecting visitors?" Doby asked.

"Go open it," Bart said, lifting the gun and pointing it at Doby. He turned toward Pamela. "Stay seated. You do anything dumb and he's dead."

Bart stayed several steps behind Doby as they walked through the entrance hall. Doby slowly opened the door and stood beside it.

"Go," someone said on the other side of the door.

Four hooded men rushed into the room. They stopped, taking in Doby standing behind the door and Bart beyond him with the raised gun and voice. "What's going on here?"

Doby stepped forward. "You came to the right place. We need your excellent services, Your Honor."

"What? What are you doing here?" One of the men asked Doby.

"Your Honor, Mr. Anarchist, we need your assistance."

"How do you know it's me?" Anarchist said.

"Please, you've been commissioned to lead a court trial. Come with me to the court room."

Anarchist and the three men carrying baseball bats walked with Doby. Bart followed, gun still at the ready, asking questions no one answered. The men arriving ignored him and his weapon.

"Who's she?" Anarchist asked as they entered the 'court room'.

"She looks familiar," one of the men said, "like Lynette."

Pamela narrowed her eyes and folded her hands across her chest.

Bart waved his gun at all of them, finally getting their attention, "What are you talking about a trial? I didn't order this."

"Bart, be patient. I just thought we could use their services to get this resolved," Doby said.

"Who's on trial?" Bart asked.

"I was thinking of a re-trial, in light of the sentencing I received this afternoon." He rubbed his fingers over the bump under his left eye.

"You can't do that," Bart said, waving the pistol at the hooded men.

"Who is he anyway?" Anarchist asked, pointing back at Bart.

Doby looked at Anarchist. "Your honor, that is Mr. Omnipresence, a Master Arbitrator. I would propose that he will co-judge the trial with you," Doby stated.

"You don't think . . . " Pamela started.

"Ms. Alden," Doby turned to her. "I would like you to meet His Honor Mr. Anarchist, a Master Arbitrator of Social Code. Assisting him are Mr. Trucker, Mr. White Cloud and Mr. FartMan, all Master Protectors."

Trucker shifted his weight back and forth, holding the bat up in the air with one hand. "How does he know our names?"

"I dunno," Anarchist said.

Doby said, "Bart, please get your mask on and let the trial begin."

Bart did not move. "Do you want to finally put us on trial or not?"

"Yeah, Whaddya wanna do?" FartMan interjected.

Bart looked around. A smile grew from the corner of his lips. He walked over to the antique cabinet and took out a hood mask. He pulled it over his head and said, "It's my game."

... **Chapter 54** ...

Trucker and White Cloud took up positions on either side of Doby and Pamela. Bart and Anarchist sat in chairs facing the defendants with FartMan at Bart's side.

"Let the trial begin," Doby said.

"Silence in a court of law," Anarchist said. "What are the charges?"

"Your Honor, I am kindly requesting a retrial," Doby announced.

Anarchist raised his hands and pointed one finger to the side of his head. "Are you nuts? Today you were sentenced and received judgment. What else do you want?"

"Justice," Doby said.

"He didn't receive enough justice," Bart said. "He needs a lot more."

Doby stood up and said, "Thank you, Your Honor, but I would like to add more charges."

Trucker and White Cloud gripped their bats more tightly and Trucker said, "He lost his marbles, let me smack him."

"Trucker, shut up," Anarchist commanded, turning toward Doby. "What are the additional charges?"

"He ain't allowed to do that," FartMan exclaimed.

"FartMan, I'm the freaking judge here," Anarchist stated. "He can add more charges to the proceedings if I tell him he can. Now what do you want to add?"

Doby looked at Anarchist, bowing slightly. "To the current charges, I would like to add one more serious charge with grave consequences." Doby wondered if he was being an idiot, but he needed to play through the logic.

Anarchist straightened up in his chair. "Go ahead. I'm waiting."

"To the current charges, I would add that I claim to be the Supreme Being of Social Code, the Prophet."

"What are you talking about?" Bart shouted. "That's blasphemous. You're out of line. I'm in charge of Social Code."

"Wait. Let him talk," Anarchist said. "I'm the lead judge here."

"No you're not," Bart said. "I created you."

"FartMan, smack him. He doesn't understand the proper hierarchy." Anarchist commanded.

"No," Doby said. "Don't hit him, we're getting off track. . . if I may kindly interject, Your Honor."

"Yeah, it's OK. Don't smack him," Anarchist turned toward Bart and said, "You go against the hierarchy of this court and I'll order him to crack your head wide open like a watermelon. Now, I want to hear the defendant."

Doby nodded to each of the Protectors and then faced Anarchist.

"Your Honor, very simply, it appears that Mr. Omnipresence sitting next to you thinks he is in charge of Social Code. I claim that I am. One of us is telling the truth, and one is not."

"That's right," Trucker said.

"Shut up, Trucker," Anarchist said. "OK. How do you prove it?"

"Who ordered you out here tonight to perform this trial? Who gave you the instructions, and whose name was on them?"

"Like always, we get our orders from Supreme Being, who also happens to be the Supreme Court Justice of Social Code," Anarchist replied.

"So the Supreme Being would have known that you were coming here?"

"Yes."

"And did His Honor Mr. Omnipresence know you were coming? I would ask you to think back to your arrival here."

"Well . . . no," Anarchist acknowledged.

"When you walked in the door, who greeted you and knew your names—Mr. Omnipresence or myself?"

"Well, you did."

"So who is the Supreme Being of Social Code?"

"You?" Anarchist asked.

"Well you can be positive of one thing. It sure isn't him." Doby took a step forward and pointed his finger at Bart.

"You mindless jerk," Bart said, grabbing the pistol on his lap and raising it.

In one quick movement FartMan swung his bat with full force, cracking it across Bart's wrist. The gun went off and the cabinet glass behind Doby's head shattered. Bart screamed, bent over and grabbed his wrist while the gun tumbled to the floor. He howled in wordless vowels then panted, "You broke it, you brainless idiot. You broke my wrist."

"He's out of line. Trucker, justice please." Anarchist commanded.

Through the hole in the hood mask, Trucker's lips curled up in a smile as he walked over and took a mighty swing with the bat, cracking it into Bart's side. Bart groaned and fell to the floor in pain. Trucker cocked the bat for another swing and Anarchist said, "Trucker, that's enough," but Trucker followed through with the bat across Bart's back. With a hollow thud, Bart flattened to the floor.

"Trucker, I said enough. Now you Mr. Omnipresence, you ain't going nowhere until this trial's over. And if you say another word Trucker's gonna whack you again."

FartMan bent down and picked up the gun lying on the floor in front of Bart.

Bart rolled into a fetal position, holding his injured wrist with his opposite hand.

"I think the case is closed your honor," Doby said. "But do you think we should put Omnipresence on trial for impersonating the Supreme Being?"

"Yeah," Trucker said.

"No-o-o-," Bart moaned. "You don't understand. You are all idiots and have no right to make these decisions."

A loud noise at the front door preceded several men who burst into the room wearing helmets and flack jackets. Behind them followed Detectives Sloan and Waleski, also wearing flack jackets tight across their broad chests.

Trucker and White Cloud dropped their baseball bats and raised their hands. FartMan raised his hands with Bart's gun aiming toward the ceiling. Anarchist rose from his chair and raised his hands.

Bart stayed in the fetal position and began to quiver, still holding his hand. Doby stood next to Pamela, his hand on her shoulder.

"What the heck is going on?" Waleski asked of no one in particular.

Sloan shook his head. "Like some kind of a weird cult."

... **Chapter 55** ...

Pamela and Doby sat next to each other on a wooden bench in a waiting area of the Boston police station. They had just had finished two hours of interrogation, individually at first, and then together.

They sat sipping cups of stale coffee while Detectives Waleski and Sloan finished some paperwork.

Bart was in a cell, and he wasn't talking. Someone had managed to get his lawyer out of bed and he was on his way to the station. The emergency room at the hospital had already put a cast on Bart's wrist.

"You set the whole thing up tonight when you were playing with your PDA in the car, didn't you—the vigilante team and everything,?" Pamela asked, swirling her coffee in its Styrofoam cup.

Doby looked at her, "I guess there was a fair amount of risk. It certainly could have gone wrong. Technology doesn't always work, and then there is the human factor."

Pamela yawned, "This human is quite tired."

Doby pulled out his PDA and looked at the time. "Two-thirty a.m."

"This has been awful," she said, setting down her coffee and rubbing her temples.

"All because I was curious to know who was generating those stupid popup ads."

She laughed, then made a face of sympathy, "You look terrible. That eye is turning black."

"At least I can see through it. It's my ribs that are killing me, and I can hardly move my leg."

"I think you need some TLC. Why don't you come over to my place and have a bite to eat?" She gently placed her index finger on his swollen eye, "And I'll put something on those wounds."

He looked at her through his right eye and half through his left eye. "You're serious?"

She smiled. "Sure."

Detective Waleski walked through the waiting area carrying a stack of papers. He looked at them and said, "Thanks for your help and cooperation. You're free to go."

"Glad to help you," Doby said.

Waleski laughed. "You didn't just help—you solved the case. But let's not tell that to my supervisors. I'm retiring in a few months and a promotion will help push up my pension a bit."

"We were mere assistants." Doby smiled.

Waleski looked at him. "You're sure about how we can find all the other justice squads in New York and LA?"

"Yes, like I said, it's all on Bart's home PC. Any of your technical guys can easily retrieve the information."

"How do you know that?" Waleski asked.

"It's all there and much more. His password is Omnipresence."

Waleski shook his head. "I won't ask."

"What about William Marder?" Doby wondered what would happen to him. And the saps like Runner who had been sucked into this game.

"We already picked him up. He is quite distraught and incoherent at times." Waleski turned to Pamela. "I'm very sorry about your colleague Fred Hauser."

Pamela hung her head. "It was pure insanity the way this was going."

"Glad we can put a stop to it," Waleski said with conviction. "By the way, are there any accounting records for DSDesign?"

"All on Bart's computer," Doby said.

"But I thought Ms. Alden was the COO. She should know."

"No," Doby said. "She was just the receptionist. Look on their website and at all the documentation on their computer files. It's all there. She wasn't even close to the financials. That was Bart. She had no significant responsibilities in DSDesign. Just answered telephone calls."

Pamela's mouth dropped open. She started to form a word then stopped.

Doby added, "Temp job while she was trying to find work as a psychologist."

Pamela looked at Doby and finally spoke, "You seem to know so much, but I'm curious to know how you knew about those three Protectors and Anarchist?"

Doby couldn't help himself, "Trucker drives a pickup truck, White Cloud once got arrested for selling crack cocaine, and FartMan works in a greasy spoon restaurant that specializes in Boston Baked Beans." He grinned.

"And Anarchist?"

"He works for the U.S. Federal Government."

"How do you know these things?" she asked, cocking her head to the side.

Doby shrugged. "I keep telling you—simple research."

Waleski shuffled his papers, then pulled one from the middle of the stack to the top, "Does DSDesign have any cash reserves? We'll probably need to block some bank accounts."

"Some accounts in the U.S. and a couple of offshore accounts, but not much in them."

"Why not?" Waleski asked.

"The cash balance is small. It seems that yesterday afternoon someone who knew the passwords to the bank accounts made fairly large donations to various charities around the world, charities devoted to widows and orphans."

"Widows and orphans?" Pamela asked.

"Yes, 'pure and genuine religion is to take care of widows and orphans and to keep oneself from being corrupted from the world.'" Doby said. "Book of James, I think."

Pamela's eyes opened wide.

"The Bible," Doby added.

Waleski frowned, looked at him then at the sheet of paper, and nodded his head. "How much got transferred out of those accounts? Millions?"

"Perhaps, something like that," Doby replied.

"Bizarre." Waleski said, shaking his head. "And tell me, how did you get us over to Strathmore's house tonight?"

"Simple. Remember my 911 program? It also runs on my PDA. I pushed a button at a certain point and knew it would take you approximately seven minutes to get there.

"Why seven?"

"That's exactly what it took earlier today—for you to get to the residence hall where the vigilante squad was trying out for the baseball team, with me as the ball."

"I see," Waleski said, shaking his head as if he didn't.

They shook hands and Doby and Pamela headed toward the front door of the police station, Doby limped and Pamela supported him, her arm around his back. As they reached the doors, Waleski yelled out, "Mr. Duclos. Just to double check . . . the address in your French passport. Is it correct?"

"Yes, but . . ." Doby reached into the front pocket of his pants and pulled out a piece of paper and a pen. He tore off a small piece of the paper, wrote something on it and handed it to Waleski. "If you need to get hold of me quickly, the best thing is to go here. My website. I haven't had time to do much with it, but I'll set up an email link."

Doby and Pamela left the police station and Waleski looked down at the piece of paper. On it was written, '**www.odby.com**.'

"Bizarre," Waleski said.

... **Chapter 56** ...

Runner sat up in his chair, anticipating playing Social Code and spending time with Angelica. He clicked on to the game's site, and immediately Angelica appeared, her beautiful blond hair translucent in the soft light. Her young body was perfect and sleek. How he wanted to touch that body like he did in his imagination.

"Hello Runner. Welcome to Social Code."

"Hello Angelica," he said.

She shifted back and forth. "How are you today, Runner?"

"I'm fine."

"It is nice to see you. I have something important to tell you."

"I'm glad. What do you have to tell me?"

"You may want to sit down."

"I am sitting down."

"That's good," she said.

"Runner, don't be angry, but I have to tell you that I have not been faithful to you."

"You what?" he exclaimed, his hands beginning to shake.

"Now, don't get nervous with your hands on the joysticks."

"But what did you just say?"

"Just what I said. In fact, there were exactly seventy-six-thousand, two-hundred and eighty-nine other players who have been seeing me."

"You mean you have not been there just for me?" His throat constricted.

"I'm sorry, but I had to be honest with you. There is something else I wanted to tell you."

"What's that?"

"My intentions have not been pure. I have been making a lot of money off of you by manipulating you to buy things."

"What? I don't understand?"

"I put software on your computer that you didn't ask for, and I monitor everything you do on the Internet. Even worse, I send you emails according to your preferences. Here are your main preferences, the things you bought because of me."

A typed list appeared on the screen, including a device to enlarge a particular part of the anatomy, photos of nude teen girls, and various perfumes 'guaranteed' to seduce the opposite sex.

Runner was stunned and sat back in his chair. "How did you know?"

"Do you want me to send this list to your family, friends or employer?"

"No. Please no."

"Then I want you to tithe more money, five thousand dollars a month."

"I don't have that much."

"I understand. I just wanted you to think how ridiculous that would be." Angelica leaned forward until her face filled the screen, "And now there's something I want to show you."

Runner couldn't help but lean toward her, hoping he had imagined the exchange up until this point. Angelica's face began to change. Into the face of . . . Gumbo? Yes. The photo that Runner had taken of him at the Buffet de la Gare, Gumbo with his NY baseball hat on top of Angelica's body.

Runner screamed, and shot back from his desk in the chair.

Gumbo's voice replaced Angelica's. "Runner, I'll be watching you."

Runner's computer automatically switched off the Social Code site, and his screen saver started. The same picture of Gumbo appeared on the screen saver, his face looking severe. Then Gumbo looked up and smiled and his face changed back to that of Angelica, her eyes red, wild and open. Dracula teeth grew from the sides of her mouth. With a crackling witch's voice she said, "I'll be watching you."

... # ...

Pamela laughed. "I can't believe you did that."

They were downstairs in Doby's computer room at the farmhouse in Switzerland, looking at the computer monitor.

Doby smiled. "Every player of Social Code will receive that screen saver, but of course without my photo. That was especially for Runner."

Pamela looked concerned. "And the players who had Lynette, you're not going to put her face on their screen savers?"

"No, of course not. I've decided to put Lynette's naked image on screensavers on millions of computers. I think the players will enjoy it."

Pamela swatted him.

Doby laughed and ducked away sideways in his chair. "Lynette will now disappear and everyone will get Angelica. By the way, they'll have to do some very tricky programming to get that thing removed from their hard drives. I set it up like a popup ad that never dies."

"You're malicious."

"No. I just saved their lives," Doby said, realizing how easy it is to become dependent on a distorted virtual reality, the danger being that it affects how you cope with the real world and its demands. Or for that matter, relying on any worldview based on inadequate pre-suppositions would only get you into trouble. Bart's 'religion game' was only one example. He knew he needed to take care, but also understood that Bart was right about one thing. When people construct belief systems that are not build on a solid foundation, it only leads to confusion and chaos.

Pamela shook her head. "How could I have so stupidly gotten involved in this?"

"There were some positive things about it all." He caught her quizzical look and continued, "You and I wouldn't have met without Social Code. Isn't that right, Lynette?"

"Don't call me Lynette." She shook her finger at him.

He grabbed her hand and held it in his own. "Why don't we go upstairs, get out a bottle of Swiss white wine and look at the view?"

"I'd love to," she said.

They walked upstairs and out onto the terrace. It was a clear afternoon and the sun reflected off the snowy peaks of Mont Blanc.

"It's magnificent," she said.

The telephone rang and Doby excused himself. He went inside and answered it.

"Doby here," he said.

"Hello, Doby, this is Stefan. I'm back from my holiday. Had a wonderful time."

"Good, good," Doby said, worried that something wasn't.

"Just wanted to thank you for the information about the business man in Germany. Extremely helpful," Stefan said.

Doby leaned against the kitchen wall. He had gotten lucky. In Boston, after buying a laptop, he had been able to get into a computer in Germany. Stefan's German business man had low levels of security in his personal accounting system and Doby found out a few discrepancies in what the man had told Stefan.

"Glad to have helped," Doby replied.

Stefan went on, "Laszlo Vartek has agreed to help me out. He's already on his way to Berlin, and he's going to meet with my German friend to present my contract. I suspect the business deal will be successfully concluded."

Doby was glad he wasn't the German business man. "Everything else OK?"

"Yes, I may need your help on another project, but everything else is fine. Talk to you soon."

Doby breathed a sigh of relief. The one million dollars was now back in von Portzer's Panama account. And the thirty thousand was back in his own account.

Doby retrieved the bottle of wine from his fridge, uncorked it, and brought it and two glasses to the terrace.

Pamela was gazing at the mountains in the distance. "Robert, I don't know how you can work in a place like this. I would never be able to lock myself down in that dark computer room with this on my doorstep."

Doby leaned on the terrace railing. "I often spend the day working on my laptop out here." He turned to look at her and paused. He looked away again. "By the way, there's something I've been meaning to tell you."

"What's that?"

"My name isn't Robert."

"What?"

Doby smiled. "Robert Duclos is not my real name."

Her back straightened. "But the credit card. You paid with a credit card and the name was Robert Duclos and not John Burton. And the passport?"

"Remember how you talked about fictitious names, how everyone is using them and how you didn't like it?" he asked, trying not to wince.

"I remember, but it's one thing to put an alias user name on the Internet, and another to have a real credit card with a fictitious name. Who are you, Robert Duclos or John Burton?"

He poured Pamela and himself a glass of wine, the golden sun lighting the liquid to the color of glowing honey.

"Lynette, I have to confess that my real name is Gumbo." He looked at her with a twinkle in those blue eyes.

"Come on, don't give me that, and don't call me Lynette."

"OK, Gumbo's not my real name, nor is John Burton. My name is Doby, at least that's what my friends call me."

"Doby?" She looked him up and down, finally smiling "You know, I like that name. It fits you."

"Well, it's the one I use and you'll just have to live with it. And there's one other thing."

"What's that?"

"I'd like to propose a toast in celebration."

He handed her a glass of wine, took the other and raised it in the air. She raised hers.

He raised his glass even higher. "To success. The popup ads are gone."

Author's Notes:

From my chalet in the Swiss Alps, I look out and see majestic snow-covered mountains, forests, and patches of green land with small herds of cows wearing their bells. My chalet rests on the hill above a quaint village with old chalets and wooden barns, some that have been there for over five hundred years.

Yet, some of the people in those chalets, including myself, have computers with broadband Internet connections. It shows that the Internet permeates our world. Like it or not, we are connected. From just about everywhere we can surf for information, order goods, trade stocks, get psychological help, play games, and unite with others . . . even commune with belief systems.

Social Code is a book about what exists, and, in actuality, it isn't so fanciful. We know how advertising bombards us through the Internet in an effort to get us to buy something. But the power goes beyond just getting us to purchase things. The Internet also has the ability to create digital communities that can be there for good and bad. It can bring us close to those who share our interests or to manipulate our minds. As Doby would advise, keep alert.

I have been very pleased by the considerable response from readers of Social Code, and by the discussion themes this book has raised. This appears to cover a broad number of topics such as the power of the Internet, dependence, manipulation, cults and psychological undertones. The diversity of discussion was an unexpected surprise for me.

If you have any thoughts on the book, I would enjoy hearing from you. Please put the words 'Social Code' in the subject of your email message, otherwise my messaging system may treat your message as SPAM. Unfortunately, as Social Code suggests, we live in a time of internet abuse. But, please do contact me. I'll do my best to reply.

Cass Tell, Switzerland
cass@casstell.com

Publisher's Notes:

There has been a significant response to the initial release of Social Code and readers have generated some passionate discussion on the underlying themes in the book. As a result, Destinée has made available various resources on Social Code, including Reader Guides for book clubs. A more formal curriculum for discussion groups is also offered. See www.destinee.ch.

Cass Tell has completed several other books, to be released in the near future. To find out the timing, please contact us at info@destinee.ch, or visit our website.

Destinée is dedicated toward the creation of thought provoking and entertaining literature. We work with authors who deal with themes of destiny and choice, who explore ideas related to relationships, institutions, beliefs and spirituality. Our goal is to produce inspiring literature that challenges the status quo, but also has a redemptive quality.

The Publisher
Destinée S.A.